WHERE SHOULD HE DIE?

WHERE SHOULD HE DIE?

Sara Woods

'Died he not in his bed? Where should he die?'
Henry VI, Act III, scene iii

St. Martin's Press • New York

Any work of fiction whose characters were of uniform excellence could rightly be condemned—by that fact if by no other—as being incredibly dull. Therefore no excuse can be considered necessary for the villainy or folly of the people appearing in this book. It seems extremely unlikely that any one of them should resemble a real person, alive or dead. Any such resemblance is completely unintentional and without malice.

S.W.

Library of Congress Cataloging in Publication Data

Woods, Sara, pseud.
  Where should he die?

  I. Title.
PR6073.063W5   1983   823'.914   83-9635
ISBN 0-312-86702-6

First published in Great Britain in 1983 by Macmillan London Limited.

First U.S. Edition

10 9 8 7 6 5 4 3 2 1

EASTER VACATION, 1974

Sunday, April 21st

I

'It's high time,' said Meg Farrell in her most judicious tone, 'that that young man found himself a wife.' It was Sunday evening and she and her husband Roger were enjoying a before-dinner drink with their friends Antony and Jenny Maitland, a frequent occurrence on that particular day of the week as it was the only one that Meg (better known to her many admirers among the theatre-going public as Margaret Hamilton) had free except on the rare occasions – all too few from her husband's point of view – when she was "resting". There had been another visitor, a younger man called John Lund, and Antony had just come back to the fireside after seeing him out.

'Plenty of time for that,' he said easily, and gave the fire a critical look but decided that it would be better untouched for the present. 'He's only . . . how old is he, Jenny?'

'Coming up to his thirty-second birthday,' said Jenny, who was apt to remember things like anniversaries.

'How time flies. It seems only yesterday . . . but I don't think his continued bachelorhood is anything for you to worry about, Meg.'

'Why not? Everyone ought to be married,' said Meg firmly. 'Jenny agrees with me . . . don't you, Jenny?'

'Yes, I suppose I do,' said Jenny slowly, so that her husband's attention was focussed on her, half in surprise and half in alarm. Jenny's serenity was one of the things he loved about her, the only thing he thought sometimes that kept him sane on the all too frequent occasions when his own capacity for stirring up trouble

7

was in the ascendant. She was disturbed now, and there didn't seem to be any reason why the mere mention of Johnny Lund should have that effect on her.

'Anyway, Meg,' he said, taking full advantage of their long friendship, 'It's nothing to do with you.'

'I don't agree with you, darling,' said Meg stubbornly. 'Men never know anything about these things. I don't think he's got over Lynn Edison jilting him, and if he found someone else—'

'I suppose that is what happened,' said Antony doubtfully.

'Of course it is. They were everywhere together immediately after—after you found out who killed Paul Granville, and then suddenly the whole thing was over and she took herself off to America.'

'Well, I admit I thought they'd make a match of it myself,' said Antony, 'but—'

'The thing is,' said Roger, 'Meg blames herself.'

'How on earth could it be her fault? That, if I may say so, is as stupid as anything I ever heard,' said Antony roundly, apparently forgetting the occasions when something similar could have been said to him, and for very much the same reason.

'They'd never have met if it hadn't been for me,' said Meg in what Antony always called her Mrs Siddons voice. 'And I like Johnny, I wouldn't have wanted him to be hurt.'

'You liked Lynn, too,' Antony reminded her.

'So I did, but I don't think she behaved very well,' said Meg.

'Well, all that's—how long is it, Antony?—about seven years ago,' Roger pointed out. 'He's had time to get over it by now. Are you going to take this case of his, Antony? He may be thirty-two, but he looks awfully young to be anyone's solicitor.'

'That's just because of your advancing years,' Maitland told him kindly. 'As for the case, I suppose I shall take it if Mallory will let me.' Old Mr Mallory was Sir Nicholas Harding's clerk, and Maitland was Sir Nicholas's nephew and in his chambers.

Roger smiled at that. 'You know perfectly well you'll do exactly as you like.'

'I've never had the trick of handling Mallory,' said Antony

8

with truth. 'But Willett can' – Willett was another of the clerks, junior only now to Mr Mallory, who for some reason had adopted Maitland's concerns as his own – 'so I'll leave it to him.'

'But it isn't exactly in your line, is it?' Roger insisted.

'If you mean it's a civil case and not a criminal one, I suppose I must agree with you,' Antony told him. 'But there isn't too much difference really . . . I mean, the law's the law.'

'A contested will,' said Meg rather scornfully.

'You must remember that I don't know a thing about this case yet except that it exists. But as Johnny's client is the person against whom the suit is being brought, I imagine it might be quite unpleasant for her if the verdict went against her.'

'Perhaps, darling, he'll fall in love with her,' said Meg hopefully. 'I don't even know her name but he did say she was very beautiful. Though of course looks aren't everything.'

'Beauty is in the eye of the beholder,' Antony agreed solemnly, but he was watching Meg with the amusement which was never very far below the surface of his thoughts. Beautiful perhaps was not a word you'd use for her, even though she had really changed so very little in all the years he had known her. Except perhaps in the way she dressed, with an unthinking and unobtrusive elegance, so that it was only rarely you noticed what she was wearing. When she'd first come to London, to make her name by a particularly horrifying rendering of the part of Lady Macbeth, she'd been the proud owner of one winter coat trimmed with rabbit fur, and a number of rather dowdy dresses, none of which her frugal nature would allow her to discard until they were worn right out. But as far as appearance went she was as slim as ever, and except when the part she was playing required a change of style she still wore her dark hair twisted round her head in a long plait. She was a little woman, four inches or more shorter than Jenny, who come to think of it wasn't a beauty either if you started to analyse her features, though he would hotly have contested such a judgement from anyone else.

'Well, I grant that's not important, Meg.' He went on. 'The real question, which I'm sure is on the tip of Jenny's tongue, is, is she

9

nice?'

'That's what counts, of course.'

'Johnny's hoping to see me on Tuesday, so perhaps I shall be able to tell you after that. Though I expect,' he added thoughtfully, 'she'll be on her best behaviour, in which case I probably shan't be any the wiser. At least, Jenny love,' he said, turning his attention to his wife, 'think how pleased Uncle Nick will be when he and Vera get home tomorrow to find me so innocently employed.'

Jenny smiled back at him with a rather half-hearted effect. Roger, who was as conscious of her uneasiness as Antony was, jumped into the conversation quickly with a change of subject.

'Where have they been this time?' he asked.

'Salzburg,' Antony told him. 'Vera has ambitions to go to the festival, and wants to spy out the land. It will be three years at the end of the Trinity term since they were married, and that's her idea of an anniversary present.'

Roger grinned. 'I hope Uncle Nick can afford it,' he said, knowing perfectly well that was the last thing likely to trouble Sir Nicholas when a question of pleasing his wife arose. 'But there's an idea, Meg. If that play of yours comes off before the summer that's something we might do.' He was a sturdily built man, not quite as tall as Antony but very near him in age. He had blue eyes and sandy hair which was straight and rather thick. A forceful personality who had also, somewhat surprisingly, the knack of effacing himself when the situation seemed to require it. Maitland could never quite reconcile his friend's occupation (he was a stockbroker) with his taste for energetic pursuits. Still the Salzburg Festival would be a nice change for Meg from being dragged aboard the *Windsong* for a stormy passage round the British Isles.

'Is the play coming off, Meg?' he asked.

'Well, darling, I don't really think so,' said Meg. She had the grace to sound apologetic, so that Antony thought immediately that she'd been raising her husband's hopes falsely on that score. 'But still I might take a fortnight or so off. It would be really kind to let Stella have a chance at the part.'

'Everybody'd be asking for their money back,' said Roger. Being known as Margaret Hamilton's husband was something that had never worried him, but he did wish sometimes that she wasn't quite so popular, so that as soon as one play came off there was another part waiting for her.

'Oh well, we'll see,' said Meg airily. 'In August, perhaps, after all it'll be all tourists then, and they should be quite contented with Jeremy's play and a look at Basil's profile. That's an idea, darlings, why don't we all go?'

'Because the tickets are an unconscionable price,' said Antony, 'and accommodation probably just as bad. Anyway I'm pretty sure you have to book at least a year in advance.'

'But you said Uncle Nick and Vera –'

'I said she was going to spy out the land, I didn't say it wasn't arranged already.' He broke off as Jenny put down her glass and got up. 'Dinner all ready, love?' he asked. 'Is there anything I can do?'

But Roger was already on his way to the door. 'I'll bring the tray,' he offered and Antony, who had not sat down again since letting Johnny Lund out but had remained in his favourite position on the hearthrug, a little to one side of the fire, crossed to the chair that was generally his uncle's and seated himself deliberately. Meg regarded him with a little exasperation, but for once in her life she did not speak her thought. They all knew perfectly well that the old injury to Antony's shoulder was very often painful and always a handicap, but it was also a fact that he hated any mention of it. Roger was one of the few people, perhaps the only one, from whom he would accept assistance. Still it might do no harm to take his mind from the subject.

'Do you really think that Roger would like that, darling?' she asked. 'I mean, I know he'd enjoy the music, but wouldn't he go mad sitting still all that time? Because it might still be possible . . .'

11

II

'Out with it, Jenny,' said Antony later that evening when he came back from seeing the visitors out. Besides his being in Sir Nicholas's chambers he and Jenny had their own quarters at the top of his uncle's house in Kempenfeldt Square. Their two floors were very far from being self-contained, but it was years now since anybody had mentioned the fact that the arrangement had once been intended to be a temporary one. Antony had had a brief, conscious-stricken period after Vera joined the household as to whether the newly-weds ought to be left alone, but fortunately he had seen the folly of that before anything irrevocable had been done.

Jenny looked at him inquiringly but did not answer immediately. She was curled up in her favourite corner of the sofa, and had as yet made no attempt to start clearing away the coffee cups and glasses, which if her husband had stopped to think would have given him a clear indication that she had expected his questions. She eyed him for a moment, her grey eyes serious, and the lamplight burnishing her brown hair with flecks of gold. 'I don't know what you mean,' she said at last.

'You've been very quiet all the evening, love.'

Jenny considered this. 'I always am quiet,' she said with some truth. 'You know I like listening.'

'Not as quiet as you were this evening,' Antony insisted. 'It was after Johnny left, I don't think you liked Meg talking about his prospects of getting married. But you know Meg, love, she doesn't gossip, she'd never say a thing like that to anyone but us.'

'That wasn't quite the point. She was right about one thing though, he's never got over Lynn Edison's throwing him over.'

'Now you're talking nonsense. He's been out with a dozen different girls since that episode, none of them very serious as far as I know, but I never had the impression he was pining for her.'

'I didn't say he was. It wasn't because she wouldn't marry him, but why,' Jenny told him.

12

'Now I'm the one who doesn't understand.'

'You see, Antony, he talked to me, one night when you were out somewhere, just after Lynn went to America.'

'You never told me!'

'No it's . . . it was very private and rather upsetting. Not that I think that Johnny would mind you knowing at all, I expect he thinks I told you ages ago. It wouldn't even have been breaking a confidence, because of course you know all about his background.'

'Yes I do, but what has that to say to anything? I hoped Johnny had forgotten all about that years ago.'

'I don't think he'll ever forget,' said Jenny seriously, 'any more than you or I have done. But I do think that until he fell in love with Lynn he'd put it all behind him quite successfully.'

'You mean that's the reason – ?'

'I'm afraid so. When he asked Lynn to marry him he told her the whole story and she said – I don't think she bothered to put it very kindly – that she was damned if she was going to marry a man with madness in the family.' The words sounded so strange from Jenny's lips that it was obvious that they were a quotation.

'But that's absolute nonsense,' said Maitland. 'Johnny is as sane as you or I. I admit it isn't a pretty story, and the poor lad heard it all from his father's own lips when he was – how old was he, Jenny, fifteen? – including the fact that his father had been responsible for his mother's death. But it wasn't as if insanity ran in the family, John Lund had a brain tumour. Surely Lynn must have realised –'

'I think we ought to do her the justice to say that she was probably worried about the effect on any children they might have,' said Jenny, who was very rarely known to harbour an uncharitable thought, much less to give voice to it. 'Johnny said he asked her to talk to you, or to a doctor if she'd rather, but she wouldn't and that was the end of it as far as she was concerned. And that's why I think he's never let himself get serious about anybody since then, I don't think it's the sort of thing he could face a second time.'

13

'If it was the right girl he wouldn't need to,' said Antony. 'And after all the trouble we went to to get that wretched girl out of trouble, including getting you kidnapped on the street and that wretched constable looking at me benevolently and saying you were probably annoyed about something and would come home when you got over it.'

'Well, she was your client,' Jenny pointed out reasonably. 'Yours and Johnny's. But I'm sorry it happened because I think he's the sort of man who needs a wife, only now I daresay he'll never let himself fall in love, really in love, again.'

'I don't know about that, these things have a habit of creeping up on you,' said Antony. 'Think of Derek and Barbara. I remember you said to me then it was just like the man in the song,' he added, smiling.

Jenny didn't pretend to misunderstand him. *'When he thinks that he is past love, it is then he meets his last love,'* she agreed. 'But don't you see, Antony, that's what I'm afraid of.'

'My dearest love, you're not thinking straight. For one thing Johnny's not thirty-two yet, you pointed that out yourself, hardly a grey-beard. And for another thing,' he added sententiously and rather tritely, 'if he meets the right girl she'll understand.'

'I hope so,' said Jenny, and got up in a determined way and began to stack the coffee cups together. 'I'm glad you're going to help him with this case,' she went on, 'only don't let him fall in love with his client this time.'

'As if one can control a thing like that,' said Antony rather crossly. 'But console yourself, love, it's hardly likely to happen a second time.'

EASTER TERM, 1974

Tuesday, April 23rd

I

Sir Nicholas and Vera had arrived home safely on the Monday afternoon, and Antony and Jenny dined with them that evening. A thing that would have been unheard of in the days before Vera's arrival: Mrs Stokes, who had been Sir Nicholas's housekeeper for as long as Antony at least could remember, confining her efforts on the Maitlands' behalf to a very ceremonious luncheon on Saturdays. But Sir Nicholas's employees had always bullied him; at least Mrs Stokes did; and Gibbs, the butler, who was old enough to have retired years ago – which everyone wished he would have done – and old Mr Mallory, his clerk who ran his chambers in the Inner Temple, both did so shamelessly. But as far as the household was concerned Vera's advent had made a good deal of difference, instead of resenting her presence quite a few concessions were made to please her, this Monday evening dinner being one of them.

Tuesday was the first day of the Easter term, and uncle and nephew had made their way to the Inner Temple together. Maitland paused briefly in the older man's room, noting the neatness of his desk which was due, as he was only too well aware, for a drastic upheaval as soon as counsel got down to work. He then paused a moment to exchange greetings in the clerk's office, and to be informed by Mr Mallory of the various engagements that had been made for him. These included a meeting at eleven o'clock with Johnny Lund and his lay client. 'Not exactly your line of country, Mr Maitland, but a very worthwhile little brief,' said Mallory. Antony thanked him solemnly, ignored Willett's wink, and went down the corridor to his own room.

The sets of papers on his desk were just as neatly arranged as those in Sir Nicholas's room had been. Willett had also taken the time to arrange them in order of urgency. Antony took a moment to be thankful that nothing had come his way that demanded his immediate presence in court, otherwise he would have had to cut short his vacation. But the first thing to require his attention would take him to the Old Bailey tomorrow, a case of aggravated assault that he had known about before the Easter break, so that before anything else he must decipher the pages of notes he had made.

If he had been given to introspection about his working habits it might have occurred to him that it was odd that he, a lover of the casual who achieved only with difficulty a suitable professional neatness, would at the end of the day leave his desk as tidy as he found it; whereas Sir Nicholas, in his person the most particular of men, would in all probability already have reaped havoc among the documents that were awaiting him. However there was time enough to worry about that later; none of the clerks would dare to try to restore order, but over the years Maitland had got into the habit of putting things straight in his uncle's room himself. In the meantime, the sooner he got down to work the sooner he would have decided whether his thoughts on the aggravated assault case before the vacation had been reasonable ones. And not for the first time he wished that his own handwriting didn't look quite so much like a Rorschach test. If anyone had ever troubled to teach him to write copperplate . . . but the idea of the ink blots had distracted him, and he wasted quite five minutes trying to decide what the scrawls he had made reminded him of, and then wondering what dreadful depravity a psychiatrist would have attributed to the answers his imagination conjured up.

Johnny Lund, who had a habit of punctuality, surpassed himself on this occasion by arriving at least five minutes early. After his talk with Jenny on Sunday evening the first thing that Antony noticed about him was how much he had grown to resemble his father, a good-looking man with fair hair, a hefty pair of shoulders and a disposition in which cheerfulness generally predominated.

At the moment though he had a serious look and his briefcase bulged ominously. Maitland, however, was too taken up with the girl his young friend had ushered into the room ahead of him to worry overmuch about the amount of reading this might presage. She was definitely a beauty, with masses of dark, wavy hair, brown eyes, and features that only just escaped being classical. She was wearing a rather severely cut navy blue coat, which perhaps accentuated her slenderness, and the thought crossed Antony's mind that this was probably not a garment of her own choosing, except insofar as she thought it would create a definite impression.

'This is Mr Maitland,' said Johnny, closing the door and coming across to her side. 'Miss Veronica Procter,' he added, and Maitland was relieved to hear no trace of possessiveness in his voice. Lynn Edison, he remembered, had been treated rather as though she were made of porcelain, but in spite of Veronica's beauty there was obviously nothing here beyond the solicitor/client relationship.

Antony acknowledged the introduction, offered chairs, and, resuming his own, waited patiently while Miss Procter looked rather disparagingly around the room, so that he half expected her to say accusingly to Johnny, 'Was this the best you could get?' After a moment he said apologetically, almost as if she had spoken, 'I'm afraid we're short of space here, but my uncle's had these chambers forever and we wouldn't have a hope of getting him to move.'

'Lawyers' offices,' said Veronica. 'I always heard . . . but that isn't the point, is it? Do you think you can help me?'

'I'm afraid, Miss Procter, I know nothing about the case yet. I think the best way to approach it would be for you to tell me your side of the story, then I needn't keep you any longer, and Mr Lund and I can go over the legal aspects of the matter together.'

'Well, I don't see what all the fuss is about. A man makes a will and leaves you all his money, that should settle it, shouldn't it? Only it doesn't seem to.'

19

'Tell me,' Maitland invited. And then, when she didn't immediately respond, 'I understand you're a nurse.'

'There's nothing wrong with that, is there?'

'A very noble profession,' said Antony, and tried not to catch Johnny's eye. 'But I need to know a little more about you than that.'

'I did my training at St Walburga's, but when I'd finished I'd had quite enough of hospitals,' said Veronica. 'Too many rules, too much kow-towing to the doctors, not to mention matron. So I thought private work would suit me best, and that's what I've been doing.'

'For how long?'

'Four years. I'm twenty-six now if you must know.'

'How many jobs of this kind have you held?'

'Three. The first was with a woman who'd had a bad labour, and the family wanted her to have some help for the first few months after the baby was born. Then there was another woman, but she really needed a companion more than a nurse. I got tired of running around after her when there was nothing really wrong, so I left. It was after that that I went to Mr Keats at Wimbledon.'

Antony looked inquiringly at Johnny. 'Samuel Keats, he died a month ago,' said the solicitor promptly. 'Miss Procter was with him for nearly three years.'

'Yes, we'll come to that in a moment. Have you any family, Miss Procter?'

'Only my sister, Fran. She's my twin sister actually. I'm staying with her now as a matter of fact, it seems it wouldn't create a good impression if I took over the house before probate was granted.'

'Miss Procter, I explained to you –' Johnny began. He sounded rather harried.

'I know all about that. Probate can't be granted until all this argument is over. But that's where you two come in, isn't it?'

'I hope so,' said Maitland rather non-committally. 'Tell me about Mr Keats and his household, you must be able to do that after being with him for so long.'

'He was an old man,' said Veronica, 'nearly eighty, and his wife, who was called Alice, had died just before I went to him. After she died their son –'

'Their surviving son,' Johnny put in.

'Yes, that's right, their son Maurice and his wife and *their* son came to live with old Mr Keats. Stephen isn't there all the time, in fact he was away when his grandfather died. He's a civil engineer, you see.'

'How old a man?'

'In his late twenties, I think.'

'Still living at home?'

'Yes, though he's engaged, so I expect that will end pretty soon. Or would have done, they're still living in the house, but of course it's mine now.'

'When the will has been probated,' said Johnny, 'and that won't be until this claim of the family's is settled.'

'We'll come to that in a minute,' said Maitland, very much as he had done before. 'I still want to hear a little more about the family.'

Veronica frowned a little. 'I don't see that it matters,' she said. 'Old Mr Keats had been retired for a long time.'

'So I suppose, but retired from what occupation?'

'He was a stockbroker.'

'A successful one, I gather.'

'Yes, very. Only you see until the courts have decided that I'm really his heir I don't know exactly how things stand.'

'Does this will that's being contested make you his executor too?'

'Yes, it does,' she told him rather defiantly.

'I see. What about the son? Maurice did you say?'

'He's a stockbroker too, running his father's old firm, and not at all hard up either.' There was a trace of resentment in her voice. 'Isabel, Mrs Maurice Keats, doesn't work, in fact I don't think she's ever had a job in her life. And if you're interested in ages I happen to know theirs, he's fifty-eight and she's fifty-five. I

21

got that bit of information gossiping with the housekeeper. Her name's Grant by the way, and she was one of the witnesses to the will.'

'The will that's under dispute?'

'Yes, of course.'

'No legacy for her then?'

'Didn't Mr Lund tell you, I'm the sole legatee?'

'I expect he did, but afterwards I couldn't remember whether he'd said sole or residuary,' said Antony inaccurately. 'How long had Mrs Grant been with the Keats family?'

'I've no idea. She's the same age as Maurice Keats, that's how the question of ages happened to come up, and she talked as if she'd been with the old man forever. Certainly she knew his wife, Alice.'

'To go back to the family living together at – Wimbledon, didn't you say, Johnny? – from what you say I imagine Stephen didn't want to follow in his father's and grandfather's footsteps.'

'No, it didn't appeal to him at all he says. I'd have thought he'd be glad to take over such a good business even if he did think it was dull, after all financial security amounts to a good deal nowadays, but he left that to his cousin, old Mr Keats's other grandson.'

'If his taste was for engineering I can imagine him wanting to follow it.'

'Oh, so can I, but to throw all that money away –'

'You said he was engaged.'

'Yes, to a girl called Sally Hargreaves. She's clever, I suppose,' said Veronica rather grudgingly, 'she has a terrific job anyway, personal assistant to the chairman of the British Iron Corporation. Though she's not anything to write home about in the way of looks, I can't see what Stephen sees in her.'

'You mentioned another grandson.'

'Julian Keats. His father was called Ralph, and I think he was a couple of years younger than his brother Maurice . . . I'm quoting Mrs Grant again. Anyway Julian's quite a bit younger than Stephen, and went quite docilely into his uncle's business.'

22

'How long has Ralph Keats been dead?'

'Ten or twelve years I think.'

'Did he leave his family well provided for?'

'I really don't know. His widow, who has the perfectly ridiculous name of Blythe, is a fashion consultant, and seems to be very successful at it. She and Julian share a flat in town, and of course her job takes her all over the place so he quite often has it to himself. Even if they felt the pinch a bit when Ralph died I don't imagine they do now. There seems to be plenty of money both in stockbroking and in fashion. More than there is in nursing,' she added resentfully.

All this time Maitland had been making a series of illegible notes on the back of a number of envelopes, originally carefully partitioned but since reduced to a tattered condition by being shoved carelessly into his pocket. 'Are there any more in the family?' he asked, looking up at his client.

'No, unless you want to include Julian's girl-friend, Jean Ingelow. She works for his mother, and sometimes goes with her abroad, but I've a pretty good suspicion that when she doesn't she stays at the flat with Julian.'

'I see. Now, Johnny, it's your turn. What is the exact position?'

'They want Samuel Keats's last will overturned, and his previous one, which he made immediately after his wife died, reinstated.'

'Who benefited from that previous will?'

'Maurice and Blythe to the largest extent, and there was a hundred thousand each for the two grandsons, Stephen and Julian.'

'Was that all?'

'Some minor legacies, to Mrs Grant for instance, and to the cook and gardener, who happen to be man and wife. The usual proviso, if they were still in his employment.'

Maitland turned back to Veronica Procter again. 'I'm not quite sure what Samuel Keats's complaint was,' he said. 'Why did he need nursing assistance?'

'You're wondering if there was a legacy for someone whose place I took,' said Veronica. 'He didn't have anyone before me.'

'The need arose suddenly?'

'Strictly speaking he didn't need anyone, any more than the woman I was with before did. He was a paraplegic, the result of an accident, the same one that killed Ralph Keats as a matter of fact. Ralph was driving the car. Well there were things he needed help with, but his wife had always looked after that, and Isabel could quite easily have gone on doing what was necessary. After all they have a housekeeper, she's absolutely nothing to do.'

'So you found your presence was superfluous. Didn't you find that rather boring?'

'It was a comfortable house and a good salary, which he could well afford,' said Veronica. 'Why shouldn't I take advantage of it?'

'No reason at all. Now about this will that's being disputed, when exactly was it made?'

'A month before he died. He asked me to call his solicitor, Mr Stanley. Of course I knew him quite well, he was a fairly frequent visitor.'

'Bernard Stanley?'

'That's right,' said Johnny Lund. 'Geoffrey's partner.'

'That's rather a coincidence, isn't it?' (Geoffrey Horton was a close friend of Maitland's, from whom he had often accepted briefs.)

'You mean because Geoffrey is my senior partner's son-in-law?' said Johnny. 'How did you come to choose our firm, Miss Procter?'

'I'd heard Mr Stanley mention your name. Mr Bellerby's name, that is. And I've never had any need of a solititor before, so short of selecting one with a pin I'd no choice but to use someone I'd heard of.'

And being the junior partner, Maitland thought, Johnny got landed with a rather tiresome client. He wasn't finding himself much in sympathy with Veronica Procter, and couldn't understand how she had ever come to take up nursing, still less to persuade an elderly patient surrounded by – presumably – loving relatives to make her his heir. But that was for later consideration. 'Mr Keats asked you to telephone Mr Stanley,' he prompted her.

'Yes, he did.'

'Did that surprise you?'

'I suppose it did a little because the occasions I'd met him before had always been when he came to dinner. But there was no reason why Mr Keats shouldn't have some business affairs to talk over with him.'

'Even so, wouldn't the normal thing have been for Mr Maurice Keats to have made the call.'

'I suppose so, but it was during business hours and of course he wasn't in the house. Neither was Stephen, and as for Mrs Keats – '

'You'd better start calling them by their Christian names, all of them,' said Maitland. 'It's too confusing otherwise.'

'Isabel then. As for Isabel, I think she was out too, but in any case she's such a scatter-brain I doubt if he'd have asked her. I'm telling you why I wasn't surprised at the time, of course after he died when I heard the contents of the will I realised he didn't want them to know about Mr Stanley's visit.'

'Had you any idea, Miss Procter, what it was about?'

'No I hadn't, in spite of what they're saying.' She was on the defensive again.

'Mr Samuel Keats hadn't told you of his intentions?'

'Not a word.'

'Did he confide them in you later when the whole thing was arranged?'

'No, he didn't do that either. I was absolutely taken aback when I heard about it.'

'About this visit of Mr Stanley's – '

'He came on a Monday, and naturally I made myself scarce while he talked to Mr Keats. But he must have arranged to come back a few days later, the will was signed on the Thursday and that was my day off and Mrs Grant and cook were called in to witness it.'

25

Maitland glanced at Johnny Lund. 'Not realising, I suppose, that that meant they weren't beneficiaries any longer.'

'If they ever knew,' said Johnny. 'I haven't talked to them yet and I think that's something that must be done.'

'You say the will named you as executor as well as beneficiary, Miss Procter. Wouldn't it have been more usual for Mr Stanley to act in that capacity?'

'He explained that to me. He said, of course if he'd been the executor he would have had to act for me when the will in my favour was challenged, but as it was he felt himself bound to the Keats family as he'd acted for them for years. So when they decided to contest the will he advised me to consult someone else.'

'Yes, I see. A difficult position for him.' Though it didn't altogether explain –

'The thing was, you see, he told me he'd argued with Mr Keats about the change, so he thought the old man was annoyed with him,' Veronica answered his unspoken question.

'Now *that* seems reasonable.'

'Well, I don't see why Mr Stanley should have cared what Mr Keats did with his own money,' said Veronica rather sulkily.

'Any reputable solicitor –' began Johnny incautiously. (At least he isn't falling in love with this one, thought Antony, allowing the humour that never deserted him for long to surface for a moment, but only in the privacy of his own mind.)

'*I* think he was exceeding his duty,' said Veronica, with a look at her own solicitor as though daring him to make the same mistake.

'Then we'd better come to the grounds on which they're contesting the will,' said Maitland in something of a hurry. 'As you described the family to me none of them is in a position to claim that reasonable provision should be made for them out of the net estate. There's talk of extending the Inheritance (Family Provision) Act of 1938 to cover more people, but as it stands at present –'

'Only Maurice could claim,' said Johnny. 'And then only if he

26

were an infant, which he isn't, or unable to maintain himself because of some disability, physical or mental. And that doesn't apply either.'

'Then –'

Johnny didn't wait for Maitland to complete his question.

'They're not claiming undue influence in the ordinary way,' he said. 'I should have explained, Antony, that Maurice Keats is taking the action to have the former will reinstated on behalf of the whole family. They're alleging fraud.'

'Against Miss Procter?'

'Yes, they say she turned the old man against them. I suppose you could say in a way that mental incompetence comes into it too.'

'But . . . did you ever discuss his family with your patient, Miss Procter?'

'Not in – in a derogatory way. Certainly not that. But of course I was alone with him a good deal and if he felt like talking naturally the affairs of the family came up sometimes.'

'But you'd not maligned them to him in any way?'

'I told you I didn't,' she said sharply.

'Well then, tell me what Samuel Keats had to say about his various relations.'

'When I first went to him – I told you that was just after his wife died – he was very grateful to Maurice and Isabel for giving up their own home and coming to live with him. And to Stephen as well, though he always said it was a pity he hadn't gone into the family business like his cousin, which I think was very unfair.'

'Come now, Miss Procter, you suggested just now that you couldn't see yourself why he hadn't done so.'

'I was thinking of the financial side of things. Besides, he wouldn't have had to spend so much time away from home. Still, it was his decision to make, I don't think his grandfather should have criticised him for it.'

'What about the other side of the family? Did he feel any resentment towards his son Ralph because of the accident?'

'No, he said Ralph had done everything possible to avoid it.

27

Somebody jumped a red light, they were to blame if anybody was.'

'Then, come to think of it, Mrs Ralph must have been reasonably well off. I suppose the other party's insurance company would have to settle.'

'I haven't been into that,' said Johnny, 'but I imagine that was the case. But go on Miss Procter, you were telling us –'

'I don't know about the money side to it, only that in spite of being crippled himself Mr Keats didn't blame Ralph. He always said Blythe was a flibbertigibbet, but when she visited the house he was . . . well, if he hadn't been so old you could almost have said he flirted with her. And he was glad, of course, that Julian had gone into the business.'

'Let's see, you said that Stephen was engaged.'

'Yes, but I may have exaggerated about that, nothing's been announced yet,' said Veronica with a sort of satisfaction in her voice that puzzled him for a moment. 'But Sally has been to the house, and so has Jean, Julian's girl friend, and Mr Keats liked them both until lately. About three months before he died he began to get a little critical of everybody. Maurice wasn't running the business properly, Isabel was always out, Blythe didn't come to see him often enough, and he was quite sure Julian would have been better in some other profession.'

'And Stephen?'

'He wasn't pleased with him either, but in a way what he said was a compliment. That if he had gone into the firm things would have been much better.'

'Were these criticisms true? The business for instance?'

'I don't really know anything about that. Maurice never seemed to be worried.'

'And the others?'

'If you mean the other things he said about his relatives, there wasn't any change really. I mean in the way they acted. Isabel had always been out a lot, Blythe couldn't come very often because she was abroad as much as Stephen was. As for Julian, that comes under the heading of business too and I haven't the faintest idea whether he was competent or not.'

'Well, the family think, or say they think, that you were responsible for these changes in the old man's attitude.'

'That's what they say. They say I ingratiated myself with him and then told him lies about them. But I didn't do that . . . ever!'

'Think about it for a moment, Miss Procter. Was anything at all ever said between you and Mr Keats that could have been overheard and construed in that way?'

'If you mean to sound as if I was trying to get round him . . . I didn't even like him. Even if I'd wanted to criticise the family I'm not at all sure he'd have taken it from an outsider. What he said himself was different, of course.'

'Yes, I see what you mean about the question of his testamentary capacity, Johnny. What does Bernard have to say about that? And whoever the doctor was?'

'Mr Stanley will confirm that he made certain complaints about his family in their first discussion of the will, but that he had no reason to doubt that he wasn't in full possession of his faculties. Dr Walton also says that mentally he was as sharp as ever.'

'What about you, Miss Procter? Did you notice any difference in him?'

'I've just been telling you that I did. But there was nothing wrong with his mind, that was as clear as ever.'

'If he died a month later, perhaps the cause of his illness, whatever it was—'

'He died from gastric influenza, but he wasn't ill at the time he arranged about the will.'

'How long did his illness last? You see, Miss Procter, Mr Lund and I have to have an exact picture of the last months of his life, because these are questions that will be asked in court.'

'Yes, I suppose so. He died two weeks ago, the week before Easter, Monday the eighth of April to be exact.'

'And he had never mentioned the change in his will to you?'

'I already told you—'

29

'Yes, Miss Procter, but I have to be very clear about this. Did he give you no hint even of what was in his mind?'

'It was a complete surprise to me.'

'Very well. You haven't told me yet how long his illness lasted.'

'About five days. So there's no question of his mind being affected at the time the will was made,' she insisted. 'But must we go over and over this?'

'I'm sorry to try your patience.' There was no hint of apology in Maitland's tone. 'I won't keep you much longer. You say you knew nothing of the new will. Was it as much of a shock to his relations, who were no doubt expecting to inherit?'

'I'm sure they knew nothing of it.'

'You say, however, that during the last three months of his life he had become – shall we say disillusioned? – with his relations.'

'Yes, he had.'

'And that seemed perfectly natural to you?'

'I thought it was just a mood and would pass.'

'Were they aware of the change in him?'

'I don't know about Mrs Blythe Keats. I'm sure she must have visited the house sometimes during that period, but it always happened to be when I was out. Julian never mentioned that he had noticed anything, and Stephen . . . I don't know about him either, he was away most of the time and only got back after his grandfather died. But the other two who were living in the house, I often heard him speak very sharply to them. And they certainly noticed it, it was quite a change from his usual manner, and I'd see them exchange glances with each other when he said something particularly unkind.'

'That is Mr and Mrs Maurice Keats? Maurice and Isabel Keats to be exact?'

'Yes, of course.'

'Very well, Miss Procter, we'll leave it there until I've had time to study the statements that I'm sure Mr Lund is about to unload on me. If you'd like to see Miss Procter out, Johnny, and then come back we could go over the matter together.'

30

Veronica Procter got to her feet. 'I don't like being kept in the dark,' she said, 'about something that is very much my business.'

Antony smiled at her. 'I thought you were tired of my questions,' he said.

'Yes, I am, because I don't think all this is necessary. There can be no doubt about it, can there? He made a will and I'm his heir and the money will come to me. All this is just a formality.'

'That's something I can't tell you at this point, Miss Procter. I really think it will be better if Mr Lund and I go into the matter together, then we can have another talk if you like. But don't think I'll be able to give you any definite assurance of a happy outcome, going to law is a tricky business, and one can never be sure of the result.'

'That's what Mr Lund says,' she agreed rather sulkily. 'And he said we should have to consider the desirability of making a settlement out of court, but that's something I simply won't consider.'

'It might be very much to your advantage.'

'I don't see that. They've all got plenty of money. Why should they want more?'

'That's an argument that might cut both ways. If satisfactory provision were made for you–'

'I won't agree to it, and that's flat.' She said goodbye rather abruptly and then turned and went out.

Johnny obviously escorted his client until he was able to put her into a taxi, because it was nearly ten minutes before he returned to Antony's room. 'Well?' he said, as he closed the door behind him.

'A difficult young lady,' said Maitland mildly. 'Come and sit down, Johnny, and tell me exactly what is being alleged. Not, I gather, that she used her wiles on the old gentleman to get him to fall in love with her.'

'No, funnily enough nobody's suggested that. They say she persuaded him that they were all plotting together to have him declared incompetent and put away in a home. I believe I mentioned mental incompetence earlier because it's the most

31

obvious thing in a case of this kind and if she'd tried to persuade the old gentleman that she was indispensable to him . . . but that isn't really what is alleged. They say that he made the will under a mistaken impression, and because Miss Procter is the gainer thereby I suppose it's natural for them to think she was responsible, and that's where the question of fraud comes in.'

'You have statements to this effect? Do they all tally?'

'Maurice's is by far the most circumstantial. Apparently on one occasion when they were alone together his father had come straight out with the accusation. But Maurice said he'd got an extremely detailed story into his head, even naming the place he thought they meant to send him, and saying that Maurice was going to ask for power of attorney over his affairs.'

'I see.'

'Isabel only knew that by hearing it from her husband, but she'd certainly noticed the difference in her father-in-law's attitude during the last few months. Their son was away at least part of the time, Miss Procter told us that, so there's no statement from him.'

'Just as well I imagine. That briefcase looks ominously dilated.'

'Not too bad,' Johnny assured him. 'Blythe – of all the God-awful names – also said she'd noticed a change in his attitude, but thought perhaps it was due to his liver. Not terribly helpful to their case. Julian, however, could back his Uncle Maurice up from his own knowledge, old Mr Keats had said to him one day something about supposing all you young people would be glad to be rid of him. I think Julian was puzzled at the time, at least that's what he says, because it was before his grandfather was taken ill and he could only think he was referring to dying.'

'I see. That's that then. When do you suppose the case will come on?'

'Not for a month or so . . . which doesn't please Miss Procter,' he added smiling. 'Have a look at all this when you have time,' – the sheaf of papers was not quite so bad as Maitland had feared – 'and then we'll get together on it again.'

32

'And no doubt you at least will have the pleasure of another talk with Miss Veronica Procter,' said Antony rather drily. 'Never mind, Johnny, you can't win them all. Let's go and see if Uncle Nick is ready to go to lunch.'

II

From time immemorial Sir Nicholas had been in the habit of dining with the Maitlands each Tuesday evening. This was because his housekeeper, Mrs Stokes, (whom her employer said cooked like an angel in the ordinary way) chose that evening for her weekly visit to the pictures, an occasion not to be interfered with any more than Gibbs, the butler's, inalienable right to retire at ten o'clock whatever the circumstances. Until Jenny took pity on him Sir Nicholas had on these occasions been faced with what he generally referred to as a cold collation, on whose horror he would even now occasionally dwell. Tuesday evening, of course, was by no means the only time when he took refuge upstairs, but it was very rarely, when they were all at home, that anything occurred to change the arrangement. Later in the evening when Roger had seen Meg safely to the theatre he would no doubt be calling in as well; the Farrells were such old friends now that even Sir Nicholas had accepted them as members of the family, which in his eyes gave him the right to speak his mind freely on any and all occasions.

Sir Nicholas's marriage to the former Miss Vera Langhorne, barrister-at-law, had changed none of the household's traditional practices except that in many ways it had made dealing with her husband's staff a good deal easier. Mrs Stokes told her friends, 'Lady Harding knows her place,' by which she meant that Vera had not yet ventured to take over her kitchen even in her temporary absences. Gibbs . . . well, as Antony said, there was no chance at this stage of changing him into a thing of sweetness and light, but he had at least condescended at last to make use of the house phone, which had been installed solely for his convenience, rather than stumping upstairs to deliver messages in person. This was a great concession, because there was no doubt at all that he enjoyed playing the martyr.

That evening the events of the short Easter vacation still gave them plenty to talk about, and it wasn't until dinner was over and they were settled by the fire with their coffee, and Antony was making the rounds with a newly-filled decanter of Sir Nicholas's favourite cognac, that his uncle, occupied with the preparation for the leisurely enjoyment of a cigar, asked casually, 'I gathered from something you and Johnny Lund said at lunchtime, Antony, that you were taking on a case for him. Does that mean Bellerby's beginning to feel a need for help with the criminal side of the practice at last?'

'Not really, Uncle Nick.' Maitland paused with the decanter in his hand the better to consider his reply. 'It's a nasty business if the girl's done what's said of her, but rather dull because there's very little that can be adduced in the way of proof that she didn't. We shall have to stick to stout denial, as Bertie Wooster would have said.' He remembered his duties and began to pour again.

'And has Johnny fallen in love with his client again?' asked Roger, who had arrived some time since.

'Not on your life. You might as well fall in love with a–a prickly pear,' said Antony. 'I've got to admit she's damned good-looking, and perhaps she can be pleasant enough when she wants. But as far as she's concerned over this affair Johnny and I are merely paid technicians, no need to put herself out to be pleasant to us.'

'She sounds horrid,' said Jenny. Perhaps it was the implied criticism of her husband that wrung from her so uncharacteristically uncharitable a remark.

'That isn't to say she's at fault in this case,' Antony pointed out, completing his task and returning the decanter to the tray on the writing-table.

34

'Not making sense, Antony,' said Vera, who had a habit of elliptical speech. 'What's this young woman alleged to have done?' Vera was tall, with a great deal of greying hair that was always escaping from the pins that were intended to confine it. She had a gruff way of speaking, and a distinctly grim smile, quite alarming to anyone who didn't know her well. Marrying late in life had changed her hardly at all, except that the sack-like dresses she generally favoured now had some style about them, and were generally of some pleasant, though subdued, colour rather than the dun shade she had always favoured.

'She's a nurse, and she's been left a great deal of money by the patient she's been looking after. A chap called Samuel Keats, a retired stockbroker. The family are trying to have the will set aside, and the previous will, made just after his wife died – also just before my client joined the household as it happens – reinstated.'

'Undue influence?' said Vera. 'If the girl's as good-looking as you say –'

'Not exactly, but that reminds me of something I've been meaning to ask you for years, Uncle Nick, though it's not strictly relevant to this matter. You had a client who was defending a similar action. You said she had a face like the back of a bus.'

'I cannot recall ever having said any such thing,' said Sir Nicholas with a slight shudder.

'Well that was what you meant anyway. What I'm getting at is, how did you convey to the jury the unlikelihood of her having influenced her patient without actually pointing out why?' Maitland asked, single-mindedly ignoring his uncle's protest.

'I appealed to their intelligence,' said Sir Nicholas with dignity. 'After all, they could see for themselves . . . but you say it isn't exactly undue influence, which I find incomprehensible. Perhaps you'll explain to us –'

'I told you she was very good-looking, so that would have been the natural thing to rely on,' said Maitland. 'The difficulty is, I think, that the testator seems to have been a very bright old man, so that the question of mental incompetence doesn't come into this in the ordinary way. They're alleging fraud.'

'In what way?'

'That somehow or other she turned her patient against his family. *She* says he started complaining about them for one reason or another three months ago. I haven't any of the exact dates in my head, but the new will was made about a month before he died.'

The cigar was ready and Sir Nicholas was taking his time about lighting it. When he was quite sure that it was drawing well he looked up at his nephew. 'I gather you don't like your client,' he said. 'Do you think she's telling the truth?'

'She may be. Or she may just think she is.'

'I think that also needs a little explanation.'

'I mean that she's the sort of girl who might quite likely have said unpleasant things about the others to her patient from time to time, though she swears she didn't. But she might have done it unconsciously because it's part of her nature, and now be telling the truth as she sees it.'

'I hope Johnny isn't under the impression that he's doing you a favour by giving you this brief,' Sir Nicholas commented.

'I'm sure he's under no illusion at all about that. But he knows me very well, and I think he felt he needed my help.' For a moment they regarded each other: two tall men with a certain likeness between them that was one of expression only. In other respects they were as dissimilar as could be. Sir Nicholas was fair, fair enough for it to be impossible to tell that there were some white hairs among the others, while Antony's hair was dark and rather springy, except when he had been in court for some hours and it had been compressed under his wig. The older man's features, too, were far more regular than those of his nephew, and his manner was unconsciously authoritative where – except when occasion demanded it – Maitland was casual. 'Not in the way of meddling, as you call it, sir,' Antony went on, rather more urgently than the occasion seemed to demand. 'I told Jenny that you'd be glad to find me so innocently employed . . . as I believe you put it once.'

36

'So I am, my boy, so I am,' said Sir Nicholas cordially. 'All the same, something about this very ordinary case is troubling you and I should like to know what it is.'

'Nothing at all,' said Antony promptly, 'except that I don't like young women with no manners. I find myself in the position of having to do my best for her –'

'It will help Johnny,' said Jenny in her quiet way.

'So it will. That's all there is to it, Uncle Nick . . . really.'

His uncle gave him a long, considering look. 'Very well. How do you propose to deal with the matter?'

'There's no hurry about it.'

'So I suppose. The question remains, however.'

'Johnny wants me to talk to the witnesses to the new will, old Mr Keats's cook and housekeeper. That's going to be pretty awkward, because they were beneficiaries under the first will and they must know by now that they've been cut out, but with any luck they'll confirm that their employer was just as usual at the time of the signing. Then there's the doctor, I gather he'll say that his patient's mental capacity was unimpaired, which is why the family have no use for his evidence.'

'And the precise nature of the allegations against this girl? Do you realise, Antony, you still haven't told us her name?'

'Veronica Procter. I told you . . . fraud. They say she got the old man to sign the new will by telling him lies about his family, that they were trying to have him moved to some sort of a home.'

'Do you know, I think they might have great difficulty in proving that. Unless they have some concrete evidence to back up the assertion. Have they?'

'I don't know yet. There seems to have been some delay, which is odd because the Keats's solicitor is Geoffrey's partner, Bernard Stanley, and you know he's as bad as Geoffrey is for wanting to get on with things. I think, to tell you the truth, that Johnny's hoping for something that will help him to persuade Miss Procter to settle out of court.'

'Best thing in these cases,' said Vera, out of long experience.

'Oh, I agree, but she's quite adamant that she won't.'

37

'You'll have to look at precedents,' said Sir Nicholas. 'The Inheritance Act of 1938 is hardly applicable in this case, but if we go back to the Statute of Wills in 1540, or perhaps still further to the reign of Edward I and the First Statute of Mortmain –'

'You're going too far, Uncle Nick,' said Antony grinning.

'Only as far as the thirteenth century.'

'And showing off into the bargain. I know you looked up all that stuff when you needed it for the talk you gave on the history of English law to the Palmers Club in America. An Act that prohibited the conveyance of land to religious bodies without licence from the crown has absolutely nothing to do with the case.'

'I always, however, thought it grossly unfair.'

'I know you're only teasing, Uncle Nick,' said Jenny, 'but it's leaving me dreadfully confused.'

'I'm sorry about that, my dear, but Antony is just as aware as I am of the need for thoroughness in these matters.'

'If you want to know what I think,' said Roger, 'it's perfectly obvious what happened.' They all turned to look at him in some surprise, but Antony reflected for perhaps the thousandth time how extraordinary it was that there were times when you could almost forget that Roger was in the room, while when he wished to assert himself . . .

'Tell us,' he invited.

'The man on the Clapham omnibus,' said Roger complacently. 'He's the chap you lawyers are always interested in, aren't you?'

'There's a somewhat outmoded convention to that effect,' said Sir Nicholas, 'but it is some time now since I heard him referred to.'

'Never mind.' That was Roger again. 'I'm just speaking in the name of common sense. How old was this chap who made the will, Antony?'

'Nearly eighty, so I'm told. And in a wheel-chair for the past ten or twelve years,' he added, because he thought he saw where his friend's argument was tending.

'There you are then, it's obvious. He got crotchety as he got

38

older, and took it out on his family. I should think they'd have a very good case on those grounds – '

'Testamentary capacity,' said Vera, who liked to get things straight.

' – rather than accusing the nurse of all this devious plotting.'

'It's a point to bear in mind certainly,' said Maitland slowly.

'But for some reason you don't believe a word of it,' said Roger accusingly. 'Oh well, my own fault I suppose for putting my oar in in front of all you legal eagles. In future I'll stay on the sidelines with Jenny.'

'I didn't mean that, it's a very good argument,' said Antony, as seriously as if he thought his friend's apology had been equally seriously intended. 'It's just that . . . well I shall know more about it presently. Meanwhile you'd better get Vera to tell you about Salzburg, in case you succeed in persuading Meg to take some time off.'

I

The aggravated assault case kept Maitland in court all the following day, but Johnny Lund – perhaps on the principle of striking while the iron was hot even though there was no real urgency – had managed to get told of his first two witnesses and was waiting in chambers with Mrs Grant, old Mr Keats's housekeeper, and a stout, nervous woman whom he introduced as Mrs Matthews, who turned out to be the other witness to the disputed will. Antony took them down the corridor to his own room, which was really much less comfortable than the waiting-room, seated them and offered tea, an offer which was gratefully accepted. Fortunately it wasn't long in coming (as far as he could remember afterwards they'd talked about nothing but the weather while waiting for it) and it had, as he had hoped, an immediately relaxing effect.

'Well, you could have knocked me down with a feather,' said Mrs Matthews, sipping elegantly, (a thing which on the face of it was very unlikely) 'when we knew that hussy had got round the old man to cut us out. Me and Bert had been with him twenty years, and Mrs Grant nearly as long. Of course when it was just the two of them and no illness in the house it wasn't so much work, but it's nearly five years now since the others came to live with him and that Mrs Isabel never lifting a finger, while as for Stephen . . . you know how young people are.'

'At least that was my complaint rather than yours,' said Mrs Grant. She was taller than her companion, a little too thin, and with delicate features. 'Not that I didn't have help when we could

40

get it, but you know how it is nowadays, mostly I had to do everything myself.'

'And picking up after Mr Stephen Keats was one of those things?' Antony asked.

'Yes, it was, not that I minded that. Being used as a kind of lady's maid by Mrs Maurice Keats was worse; but there, a job's a job as they say and Mr Keats had always promised I'd be well looked after.'

'That's just what he said to me and Bert,' said Mrs Matthews triumphantly. 'But cooking for five people is a bit different than cooking for two, especially when one of them's a nurse and that particular. And she persuaded him –'

'Forgive me, Mrs Matthews. That kind of speculation is something that neither Mr Lund nor I can enter into at the moment. What I need from you two ladies is a description of the signing of Mr Samuel Keats's latest will. Perhaps you'd like to start, Mrs Grant.'

'Mr Stanley, that's Mr Keats's solicitor,' she explained, 'had made two daytime visits not very far apart. The second was on March 7th, and I remember that it was a Thursday because that was Miss Procter's day out. After he'd been with Mr Keats for a while Mr Stanley came downstairs to find me, and also asked Mrs Matthews to go with us. When we got upstairs he explained it was Mr Keats's will we were to witness, that we were to watch him sign and neither of us were to leave before we'd put our names to the – the attestation clause he called it, to say we were witnesses.'

'You were told nothing of the contents of the will?'

'No, and I didn't expect to be. I thought it was some slight change he'd decided on, none of my business.'

'Then you didn't know that as witnesses you were debarred from inheriting?'

'No, I didn't know that, not till Mr Stanley explained it after Mr Keats was dead. It was rather a blow, I have to admit that, though Mr Maurice Keats says I can stay on, and he said the same for Daisy here. But I'll be getting my pension soon and I thought with a little extra I could go and join my sister at the seaside. That won't really be possible now.'

'Have you anything to add to that, Mrs Matthews?'

'No, not a thing. She's educated is Mrs Grant,' she added in a confidential aside, 'understands these things better than I do. But I must say it was a dirty thing to do after all these years, and if that hussy hadn't twisted him round her finger – '

'Have you ever seen or heard anything that might confirm that impression of yours, Mrs Matthews?'

'No, no I haven't,' she said with obvious reluctance. 'But how else could it have been?'

Mrs Grant was smiling. 'You'd better be careful, Daisy,' she said. 'Mr Maitland and Mr Lund are lawyers, and Miss Procter's lawyers too, and if they get you into court – '

'Get me into court? I haven't done nothing wrong.'

'Of course not, Mrs Matthews.' It was time, Maitland reflected, for a little soothing syrup. 'But you do understand, don't you, that that's where this affair will probably be settled, and it's very likely that Mr Lund will need your evidence. And Mrs Grant's, of course.'

'Well now!' It was obvious that the suggestion didn't altogether displease her. 'And what would you be wanting me to say?'

'The truth, the whole truth and nothing but the truth,' said Maitland lightly, hoping that she would have come across the phrase somewhere and that its familiarity would reassure her. 'Had you seen any difference in Mr Keats in, say, the three months before he died? Any difference in his attitude towards you or towards his family?'

'To tell you the truth I didn't see that much of him. About once a month he'd come to the kitchen – he was in a wheelchair you know – when he knew Bert would be having his elevenses, and he'd chat with both of us, tell Bert how well the garden was looking if it was summer, tell me he thought my steak and kidney pie was getting better every year, things like that. No, there weren't no difference in his attitude to us, and

42

of course I didn't see him with the other members of the family.'

'How long before he died was it you last saw him?'

'Well, I don't remember exactly, but it was quite a while before we witnessed the will. And if I'd known what it meant me having to sign it I would have given him a piece of my mind there and then.'

'How did he seem that day?'

'Serious-like. He was always one for a joke, you know, but then at his age a thing like signing your will would make you think.'

'Serious, but otherwise just as usual? No sign of any sort of mental disorder?'

'If you mean was he in his right mind, of course he was. That's what makes it so bad, what he did to us.'

'Thank you, Mrs Matthews. Could you give me your impressions, Mrs Grant?'

'Your first question concerned the last three months of his life, didn't it? Of course I saw him quite frequently, and I must say he didn't seem quite himself. A little more thoughtful than usual, that's the most I can say. And sometimes he seemed to be watching the others, I can't explain that either, except that it wasn't quite like him.'

'What was his relationship with Miss Procter?'

'I think he appreciated the care she gave him, she's obviously a very good and conscientious nurse and she didn't have that falsely cheerful air that some professional nurses acquire, calling the patient "we" and . . . jollying him along as you might say.'

'Did you like her, Mrs Grant?'

'I don't think that's quite a fair question, Mr Maitland. I was in what she obviously considered a subordinate position, something I've not always been used to, and I think I may very easily have taken offence when none was intended.'

Maitland smiled at her. 'If you were asked in court about Mr Keats's mental competence immediately preceding the making of his will and on the day on which you witnessed his signature, what would you say?'

'I'd say he was growing older and perhaps a little tired. He'd been in that wheel-chair for nearly twelve years, you know, and though after so long we'd all got used to it . . . it's a big house, and they had a lift put in so that he could go and come as he liked, but still it must have been irksome to him sometimes. But that was only the physical side, mentally he was as sharp as ever he was. And the day he signed his will he was serious, as Daisy says, but after all it was a serious occasion. To tell you the truth, Mr Stanley was the one who seemed uneasy.'

'And you have never, either of you, seen anything to suggest that Miss Procter was endeavouring to influence him in any way.'

'I daresay she did, but I'd no means of knowing it,' said Daisy Matthews belligerently.

'Mrs Grant?'

'No, quite honestly I didn't see anything either to suggest such a thing.' She smiled herself then. 'If I must be truthful I'd very much like to be able to tell you something different. Daisy and I stand to gain, and Bert of course, if the new will is upset. I don't understand at all why Mr Keats made the change but it wasn't because he was going mad, and I can't say anything different.'

II

When the two women had gone – Johnny had shown as much solicitude in finding them a taxi as he had the previous day for his client – Antony looked up rather ruefully from the notes he had been making and asked, 'Well, what do you think of that?'

'If you made anything useful of it, that's more than I did,' said Johnny.

'That's just what I meant. We were talking about it last night and Roger thinks it was all perfectly natural, Samuel Keats was getting old and a little testy, and it isn't unprecedented for people to turn against their nearest and dearest on those occasions. And

44

I suppose, since the two ladies that have just left had been with him so long, they were included in the general displeasure.'

'It sounds the most likely thing certainly,' Johnny agreed.

'Yes, but it leaves one big question. Why did he pick on Veronica Procter as a substitute?'

'It's a puzzle. Of course I suppose she was at least reasonably polite to him,' said Johnny consideringly.

'Yes, I suppose so too. But one thing's very clear, the family hasn't the faintest hope of proving that she influenced the old man.'

'Only what he said himself.'

'And whose word do we have for that? Only the people who stand to gain by the new will being set aside, Maurice Keats in particular.'

'I see what you mean. Do you think there's any point in seeing the doctor?'

'I think you should see him certainly, but I don't think we've anything to worry about really, so unless anything spectacular arises out of his evidence there doesn't seem much point in my doing so too. All the same I don't understand why the family didn't rely on straight mental incompetence, without the complicating factor of our client's fell hand in the business. Bernard Stanley is a very competent lawyer, Geoffrey wouldn't have gone into partnership with him otherwise, and he must have advised them on that point.'

'Spite,' said Johnny simply. 'If they were counting on the money and suddenly found they weren't going to get it, wouldn't they feel spiteful about the person who was put in their place?'

'Perhaps I'm making too much of it. The common sense answer is obviously the right one.' Maitland, in spite of his words, did not sound at all convinced.

'Anyway,' said Johnny, anxious to bring his companion round to his way of thinking, 'fraud and deceiving the testator would certainly be held as sufficient grounds for setting the will aside.'

'I know, but if the jury aren't convinced that our client had anything to do with the making of the will in her favour–'

45

'Then the family fall back on what you said in the first place, mental incompetence. I agree with you, Antony, that's where their real opportunity comes in, and that's what we have to think about countering.'

Antony glanced down at his notes again, picked up a pencil and began to write. 'As far as I remember,' he said, 'for the purposes of making a will a person will be judged as of unsound mind in the legal sense if they suffer from a delusion of some sort, or believe to be true things which an ordinary person wouldn't credit. Maurice Keats may be right, and his father believed that the family were trying to railroad him into an institution, but is it so unlikely that that's exactly what they would have liked to do? A jury may believe what Maurice said his father told him, without believing that it was a delusion or that the old man was legally insane.'

'And where the mental capacity of the testator isn't in question,' said Johnny, 'it'll be presumed that he knew exactly what he was doing.'

'Precisely,' said Maitland, in an unconscious imitation of his uncle's manner. He put down his pencil again and looked up at his young friend. 'Go and see the doctor, Johnny,' he said, 'and let me know what he says. Also, of course, let me know when you hear from Bernard Stanley. Then we can discuss whether it's worth while having another attempt at getting our client to settle out of court. It seems that at the moment we can't honestly advise her it would be to her financial advantage to do so, but I can't help feeling that would be the fairest thing.'

'That's because you don't like her,' said Johnny, who seemed determined that day to follow Roger's example and represent the voice of reason. 'Well, neither do I,' he admitted. 'But I suppose we mustn't allow it to influence our judgement.'

Antony glanced at his watch. 'It's getting late, but I think I'll walk home anyway,' he said. 'I hope you haven't to go back to the office again this evening.'

'Well, only to freshen up before a dinner date,' said Johnny cheerfully. 'It's quicker than going home.'

46

They parted in the Strand opposite the Royal Courts of Justice. Antony was thinking as he went that that remark of Johnny's would amuse Uncle Nick. He had advised so often, don't get personally involved in the affairs of your clients; and here he was allowing prejudice to sway him, but in quite a different way. But there was an uneasiness at the back of his mind, unadmitted even to himself, that was to stay with him for many days to come.

Saturday, April 27th

I

Another family tradition, that Antony and Jenny should lunch with their uncle and aunt each Saturday, was not so religiously observed as the Tuesday night dinners. But it was a useful occasion for the exchange of information and therefore took place whenever they all were free. Jenny was naturally not a very talkative person and with three lawyers in the family had long since got used to legal shop being talked over the meal, at least when Gibbs could be persuaded that they were quite capable of serving themselves. On this particular day, however, he was in one of his martyred moods, a martyrdom which he thoroughly enjoyed, and insisted on remaining in attendance until the last crumb had been eaten.

But once the coffee had been served in the study, always Sir Nicholas's favourite room and in fact the only one that was now available since Vera had re-arranged the big drawing-room as a music room, the old man did at least condescend to leave them. Sir Nicholas, who these days was inclined to pick and choose among the briefs offered to him, hadn't been in court so far this term but was studying in a rather desultory way a number of matters that would be coming up for trial before too long. He demanded and received an account of the aggravated assault case, told his nephew that it had been grossly mismanaged, and interrupted Maitland's protest that after all this was one occasion on which he had won a favourable verdict to inquire languidly about Johnny Lund's client.

'On the face of it,' Antony told him, 'there doesn't seem to be a

48

case to answer. The old man may have been suffering from the delusion that his family were trying to get him put away in a home, but there doesn't seem to be any evidence that Veronica Procter had anything to do with it. And you know, that's something a good many of the jury could understand and sympathise with, but still think that it was probably true. That would make only one verdict possible, even if they felt it was bad luck on the family.'

'There is also the matter of testamentary capacity,' said Sir Nicholas, 'as Vera reminded you the other evening.'

'Even if he believed that, it wouldn't necessarily invalidate the will,' said Vera. 'Too likely that it was true, as Antony says.'

'In any case,' said Maitland, 'Neither Johnny nor I have seen any of the family, of course, but other people seem to be unanimously of the opinion that he was perfectly sane. Johnny went to see the doctor, but we were pretty sure in advance what his evidence would be, or obviously the family would have been calling him themselves. As a matter of fact Bernard Stanley had consulted him in the interval between taking instructions for the new will and taking it back for Mr Keats's signature. Mentally and physically he had given the old boy a clean bill of health, and he repeated that opinion to Johnny, though Johnny says he looked at him rather strangely as he did so.'

'Don't see that,' said Vera. 'Perfectly natural he should want to see him.'

'Yes, that's what I thought, and I can't explain it either. What's still more odd, though, is that no documentation has come in so far from Bernard. We haven't had much to do with him, Uncle Nick, because Geoffrey handles the criminal side of the business, but he's told me a hundred times how punctilious Bernard is.' And at that precise moment the telephone rang.

The instrument stood on the desk near the window. Sir Nicholas said resignedly, 'I wonder which of us that is for, my dear,' but was on his feet and crossing the room before Vera had a chance to offer to find out. A moment later he returned, holding out the receiver to his nephew. 'It's for you, Antony. Geoffrey, I think, he sounds out of breath.'

'What now?' said Antony, almost as resignedly as the older man had done. Geoffrey Horton was an old and valued friend, but if he was ringing up with some urgency, as it seemed from Sir Nicholas's description he must have been, it generally meant that he had a brief in mind and probably a tricky one at that. 'Hello Geoffrey,' Maitland said, smiling at his uncle as he took the receiver out of his hand.

'I thought I'd find you there,' said Geoffrey, who not unnaturally knew their habits well enough. 'I've been arguing with myself ever since yesterday whether it would be a breach of professional ethics to call you, but damn it all, Antony, I know I can trust you by now.'

'I hope so,' said Maitland, a little startled, because he couldn't think what this rather strange opening might be leading to.

'It's just that . . . well, I thought I ought to warn you,' said Geoffrey. 'It's this disputed will where you're acting for the heir, and Bernard is acting for the family. I think you ought to know that it's just about turned into a murder case.'

II

It was almost ten minutes later when Maitland rejoined his family round the fire and all of them had long since stopped pretending that they weren't listening to his conversation. It was Sir Nicholas who broke the silence. 'Well?' he inquired as Maitland sank down on the sofa beside his wife.

Antony had had time to recover from his initial surprise. 'You were wrong, Uncle Nick, it wasn't breathlessness, it was the pangs of conscience that he was suffering from.'

'Don't tell us Geoffrey's murdered somebody,' said Jenny incredulously.

'Nothing like that, love, not a personal matter at all. In fact, nothing with which he has any professional connection. He said I

50

could tell you though, but when I hear about it through proper channels I've got to pretend to be surprised.'

'Tell us what?' said Sir Nicholas, no longer in the least bit languid.

'Something that Bernard told him.'

'Might as well tell us instead of keeping us in suspense,' said Vera. 'If it concerns Mr Stanley it's obviously this case about the will.'

'Yes, I'm afraid it is.' He glanced at his uncle. 'You know I thought we'd have a clear run, but there were things that puzzled me about it. Geoffrey's just explained them – well most of them – pretty well.'

'We have the afternoon before us,' said Sir Nicholas, leaning back deliberately and picking up his cup.

'You remember Samuel Keats?'

'The old man who died and left his money to his nurse,' said Vera, and did not add, "Don't ask silly questions," though from her tone she might as well have done so.

'He had two sons, and the surviving one, Maurice, is taking the action to try to upset the new will. The death certificate said gastric influenza, and it wasn't until several days after the funeral that Maurice went to Bernard Stanley and said he'd been thinking things over and was beginning to have serious doubts about the cause of death. After all, his father had been perfectly well, and now he had died only a month after changing his will. Well, you know that Bernard was worried anyway about the change, as any solicitor would be, even after he'd talked to the doctor; and if there was anything in what Maurice said it would lend colour to the family's claim that Miss Procter had used some sort of fraud to get the will changed. Not merely by saying that they were trying to put him into an institution perhaps, but even by telling him that there was a plot to poison him. There was still no proof of anything, but he went to talk to the doctor again and heard a more detailed description of Mr Keats's health during the last month of his life. He'd complained of some cramps, but he'd always been so fit the doctor thought it might be a vitamin

51

deficiency, which apparently would explain what was happening, and prescribed B-Complex for him. There were also a couple of bilious attacks, nothing serious apparently, which weren't a thing he'd ever suffered from but the doctor thought that his – let's say his internal workings were changing as he got older. So when the final illness came he just thought the 'flu had gone to what was now the old man's weakest part, and had no qualms at all about signing the death certificate.'

'Did he know about the will?' asked Vera pertinently.

'Not at that stage, why should he? Well, Bernard thought it over and he doesn't like coincidences any more than I do. So finally he went to the police and put the whole thing to them. The long and the short of it was that an exhumation order was applied for. There was no difficulty about it, of course, the family were only too willing and Veronica Procter, heir or no heir, needn't be consulted. The result of the autopsy came through yesterday, he was full of arsenic. Which, as I'm sure you're about to point out, Uncle Nick, is quite another ball game.'

'I always said it was a mistake for you to go to America again,' said Sir Nicholas coldly. 'Has Johnny heard of this?'

'I don't know, and there's nothing I can do about it, I've got to wait until he tells me.'

'And when he does?'

'It isn't a foregone conclusion, Uncle Nick. The family say they knew nothing of the change in the will, and if the old man looked like living forever and one of them was in a hurry for his inheritance –'

'You said yourself you don't like coincidences.'

'No, I don't. I'd give a good deal to know what's going on though. Even if she isn't arrested . . . and she's an intelligent girl, if she did it it won't have been obvious.'

'Motive,' said Sir Nicholas, 'and opportunity.'

'Not enough . . . don't you think?'

'Most murder cases are settled on circumstantial evidence.'

'That's true.' Antony hesitated a moment and divided a smile impartially between his companions. 'If the disputed will gets into court,' he said, and there can be no doubt that his intent was to annoy his uncle, 'this should add a little spice to the arguments . . . don't you think?'

III

Roger Farrell joined them for dinner that evening, instead of having a snack with Meg before she went to the theatre. They had just finished their meal and he was helping Jenny clear away when a light tap on the outer door announced Johnny Lund's arrival.

Both Roger and Meg were interested in Johnny, as being in some sense a protégé of their closest friends, the Maitlands, though they knew nothing of his past history. Tonight it took no more than a glance to convince all three of them that the young man was seriously disturbed. 'Like a cat with its fur rubbed the wrong way,' said Jenny, but that was much later in the evening.

'You're just in time for a drink,' said Antony. 'Come and sit down.'

'Yes . . . well . . . that would be welcome.'

'What can I get you?'

'I don't . . . scotch perhaps.'

Jenny interrupted at this point. 'Have you had anything to eat?' she demanded.

'Well no, as a matter of fact I haven't. You see this business with Veronica Procter is getting much more complicated than I thought, so I felt it was only fair to let you know straightaway.'

'You've heard from Bernard at last,' said Antony.

'Yes, and I understand now why there's been all the delay. But –'

'I'm going to put the remainder of the shepherd's pie back in the oven,' said Jenny firmly.

'And if it's business I'd better make myself scarce too,' said Roger.

53

'I wonder if there's anything on television,' said Jenny. 'We could watch in the other room.'

'I didn't know you had a television,' said Johnny, rather as though it was something that really mattered. Antony put his finger to his lips.

'Officially we don't,' he said. 'I think Uncle Nick would drive the pair of us out into the snow if he knew, but there are a few things we want to watch so we keep a portable set in the cupboard. Vera knows, of course, but she won't give us away.'

'Anyway,' said Johnny, 'I don't want to drive anyone out of the room. Jenny always knows all about your cases, Antony, and from some things you've said I've a good idea that Roger does too.'

'If they're interesting,' Antony agreed.

'Or worrying,' said Jenny.

'I don't think this is particularly worrying,' said Johnny, 'but as I said it's a good deal more complicated than I thought. I'd better tell you what's been happening –'

'Not until I've turned the oven on again,' said Jenny, but she was back in a very few moments. 'All right, Johnny, now you can tell us,' she invited.

'It started this afternoon when I got a telephone call from Veronica Procter,' said Johnny. 'She said the police wanted to talk to her and she couldn't think why. I said, of course, not to worry, this business about the will was nothing to do with them, even if fraud was alleged there was absolutely no proof. Still she said she'd rather I was there, so I went round to the flat she shares with her sister at four o'clock and – good lord, I've never seen anything like it before – there were the two of them and no way at all of telling one from the other except the way they were dressed.'

'They're twins, Veronica told us.'

'Yes, but I didn't realise that even identical twins were quite so much alike. Anyway the other girl – Veronica calls her Fran – went to make us some tea, and Veronica cross-examined me pretty closely about the exact legal implications of the allegations

54

which had been made against her and I tried to persuade her that she'd nothing to worry about. Only it seems I was wrong.'

'Go on, Johnny, you can't leave it there,' Antony urged after a rather long pause.

'I don't think I'm telling you this very well,' said Johnny. 'It was about five o'clock when the police were due and I admit I was pretty puzzled about what they were doing in the affair. Fran went to let them in, and I've never been more surprised in my life than when I saw who they were. It was Chief Inspector Sykes and another detective I didn't know, whose name was Mayhew.'

'Whose business is murder,' said Antony in an explanatory way, but neither Roger nor Jenny was in need of the information.

'Yes, I knew that because I've heard you speak of Sykes, as well as meeting him here once. Wouldn't *you* have been surprised?' Johnny demanded.

'Oh, I am. What did they want anyway?'

'To question her about Samuel Keats's death. You see . . .' He went on into the explanation that Antony had heard before from Geoffrey.

'I see,' said Maitland thoughtfully when he had finished. 'She was his nurse, so naturally they wanted to see her, but how seriously are they taking what the family has to say?'

'I don't know. They did ask an awful lot of questions, and you know she hasn't an – an ingratiating manner. It's a funny thing, you know, the other girl is quite different, and she kept trying to persuade her sister to be a little more conciliatory.'

'Did they warn her?'

'No. A few preliminary questions, Sykes said. And he was very glad she'd had the forethought to call me in . . . I expect you know his way.'

'I do indeed. Well now, what had she to tell them?'

'I ought to have said that what I told you came out piecemeal, not in a connected narrative. For instance . . . well, I'll tell you. They wanted to know first about Mr Keats's health ever since she'd taken him over as a patient, and she explained the nature of his injuries, that he couldn't walk but was so used to propelling

55

himself around in a wheel-chair that it didn't seem to worry him very much any more, except that he was more dependent than he liked on her. And if they were still afraid that he wasn't all there mentally she could assure them they were wrong, while as for his health it had been in general very good though he did suffer rather frequently from bilious attacks.'

'Right from the beginning?'

'That's what she said.'

'Did she report them to the doctor?'

'No, she said Mr Keats didn't want her to. He made very light of them and said it was something that had happened all his life and nothing to worry about.'

'The doctor knew about the later ones, surely, during the last month of his life,' said Maitland, making the words a question.

'Yes, and I don't like the implication of that any more than you do, but neither Veronica nor I knew the details of his statement at that point. Sykes saved it as as sort of *bonne bouche*, after Miss Procter described the exact course of the old man's last illness. Apparently that tallied well enough with what the doctor had told them.'

'So how was it left?'

'Completely in the air. There seems to be no doubt that Mr Keats was poisoned, but our client isn't the only person who could have done it.'

'No, but the best qualified. There's also the time element. A healthy old man makes a will and he's dead in a month. Besides, there are these earlier bilious attacks, quite frankly I don't believe in them.'

'Nor do I really. Nor, I think, did Sykes or Mayhew. But I can't see that they've got enough evidence to back an arrest.'

'If they're looking in the right place the evidence is very likely to turn up,' said Antony. 'All we can do is wait and see. Did you put the question of settling out of court to her again?'

'Yes, but she still wouldn't agree.'

'Very typical, I should say, but I can't see why you're

getting into such a lather about the affairs of a client you don't particularly care for.'

'The person who's accused is never the only one who suffers,' said Johnny.

'No, that's true.' Antony carefully avoided catching Jenny's eye, but perhaps the same thought was in both their minds for she got up rather quickly.

'I'll go and see if the shepherd's pie is warmed up yet,' she said.

IV

Johnny ate his belated supper with a good appetite, but left not long after he had finished. Either the food or the drink seemed to have had a calming effect on him, but Maitland was still puzzled when he came back into the living-room from seeing the visitor out and immediately Roger echoed his own thought.

'The thing is,' he said, 'if the police interview was at five o'clock or thereabouts, it surely can't have gone on for three hours or so. I know he was giving us an abridged version but all the same . . . unless, of course, these two girls he was talking about live a long way out of town.'

'I believe Frances Procter has a flat in Chelsea.'

'Not too far from us then,' said Roger. 'So why in the world didn't he get here sooner?'

'He told me once,' said Jenny, 'that walking cleared his thoughts. That seems perfectly reasonable, because I know Antony finds the same thing.'

'Yes, but what are *you* worrying about, Antony?' Roger insisted. 'I can see you're more disturbed than you should be on the face of it.'

'The same thing that I think is worrying Johnny . . . the fact that perhaps with this medical evidence our quiet civil case will turn into the equivalent of a trial for murder,' said Antony.

'That's not Johnny's line, and I know he doesn't like it, but it would be terribly prejudicial for him to refuse to represent Miss Procter now.'

'I think he's fallen in love again,' said Jenny rather dolefully. And added when the two men looked at her in surprise, 'You said yourself the girl's a beauty, Antony.'

'But a prickly one. Oh, I see,' he added, enlightened, 'you mean with the sister.'

'They're identical twins he said, so she must be good-looking too. And if she has a nicer disposition . . . oh dear, I do hope that isn't what's happened.'

'Meg thinks it's high time he was married,' said Roger.

Jenny didn't appear to find such consolation in this reminder. 'But if the other one, your client Antony, really murdered the old man to get his money . . . it's getting awfully complicated,' she complained.

'Nothing is proved yet, and perhaps it never will be,' said Maitland. 'Is that your first reaction, love, to think she must be guilty?'

'It seems awfully obvious to me.'

'Unless –' said Roger. 'When was he taken ill, Antony?'

'I've got the date in my notes in chambers, and if I look at a calendar perhaps I can remember. Thank you,' he added, as Roger pulled out his wallet and produced a small plastic card with an advertisement on one side and a complete record of the months of 1974 on the other. 'On the third of April,' he said after a moment.

'And when did Miss Procter take her days off? Somebody else must have been in attendance on those occasions.'

'That won't wash, I'm afraid, she still had the best opportunity. The third was a Wednesday, and normally she takes her day off on Thursdays, but I remember Johnny telling me that she stayed with her patient that day.'

'And he was ill for five days,' said Jenny. 'I expect the doctor visited him regularly, but she'd have control of all the medicine the old man was given. I'm beginning to think the prosecution

58

would have a very good case if it came to trial.'

'If Meg said that,' said Roger, amused by this sudden incursion into matters she generally left to others, 'Antony would accuse her of wanting to play Portia. But I'm beginning to think you're right. As a lawyer, Antony, you may see gaps in the case, but the members of the jury won't be lawyers.'

'The voice of reason again,' Antony grumbled. 'I hadn't thought about the time element before, and I'll have to look up arsenic poisoning again, but if it can be proved that no one else had regular access to him during those five days . . . even from a legal point of view I'd have to agree with you.'

'If Meg were here,' said Roger, from whose thoughts his wife was never very long absent, 'she'd be accusing you at this point of hypocrisy, or something very like it, in undertaking the defence.'

'I used to think like that,' said Jenny, 'but I understand better now.'

'Well, so do I, but –'

Maitland didn't allow his friend to finish. 'She's innocent until she's proved guilty,' he said. 'Of course, if she told me that she'd done it . . . well, I'm an officer of the court and my first duty is to the court. I couldn't put forward a misleading plea. But unless that happens – and even if she is guilty I don't think it will because she's not the sort of person to give in without a fight – I've no right to judge her. And even if all that weren't true I couldn't desert Johnny. He'll need all the help he can get.'

'No, of course you couldn't,' said Roger seriously. 'He's quite inexperienced in this sort of thing, isn't he?' That wasn't quite what Maitland had meant, but he let it pass. 'All the same –'

Roger's sentences seemed destined to remain unfinished. 'Your nice quiet case may turn into quite a sensation,' said Jenny. 'I can't think what Uncle Nick will say.'

They had only to wait until the following afternoon to find out, when Sir Nicholas and Vera, as well as Meg and Roger were taking tea with them. Later the Hardings would be going to a concert and dining out afterwards, whereas the Farrells would spend the evening in Kempenfeldt Square.

'So you think the young woman will be arrested?' said Sir Nicholas when Antony had finished a brief account of Johnny's visit the evening before. 'I hope you won't insist on meddling in the affair.'

'As to whether they'll go as far as that . . . who lives may learn,' Antony told him. 'In any case, accepting a brief is hardly meddling, Uncle Nick, even in your definition,' he added mildly.

'If that were only the end of it,' said Sir Nicholas, sighing.

'Well, it would be in this instance. For one thing, I haven't the faintest idea what could be done until I know the strength of the prosecution's case. For another, I don't intend to do anything beyond studying my brief, and perhaps giving Johnny a hint or two if he gets out of his depth. I'll do the best I can, of course, in court . . . but we're doing what you always condemn so, Uncle Nick, theorising ahead of our data. She hasn't been arrested and, as I said, we don't know that it will ever happen.'

'It seems very likely,' said Vera in her gruff way.

'Very likely,' her husband agreed. 'And if I had a pound for every time Antony's told me, "This is just an ordinary case", I'd be a rich man today.'

'But Uncle Nick, that was when he really believed that his

clients were telling him the truth,' Jenny protested.

'Generally on very slender grounds or no grounds at all.' Sir Nicholas was not to be diverted from his grievance. It was Vera who wrenched the conversation rather forcibly into different channels, and the subject was not referred to again until the four younger people were alone together and the dinner things had been cleared away.

'I ought to have asked you this last night, Roger,' Maitland said then. 'I imagine you know the Keatses, don't you?'

'The two who are in the firm, though neither of them well. Maurice is a good deal older, and Julian a great deal younger than I am. Samuel, of course, was before my time, but he's still quite a legend in the City.'

'He built up the firm?'

'He certainly did. There are rumours that he was a multi-millionaire, but he's also said to have had a very charitable streak in him. Which, come to think of it, Antony, makes it all the more puzzling why he should have chosen this Miss Procter, who doesn't sound altogether a sympathetic character, as his heir. Even if he wanted to cut out the family, surely he would have chosen some cause near to his heart to benefit.'

'The only explanation that leaps to the mind is that she really was trying to influence him. But what I was really wondering was whether the fortunes of the firm he'd built up had failed a little after his guiding hand was removed.'

'I've never heard anything to suggest it. Maurice worked for his father for many years before Samuel retired, and I think the general impression is that he was pretty well imbued with his ideas. I don't know whether Julian takes after them, unless his choosing to join the family firm is an indication that he has some ability in that direction. But in any case he's hardly in a position at his age to influence matters.'

'So you don't think they were in urgent need of money to keep afloat?'

'I suppose pretty well everyone could do with a financial shot in the arm these days,' said Roger, who was one of those few and fortunate people who had never in his life had to worry about money. Perhaps that was why, Maitland thought, his friend had never felt the slightest resentment at Meg's considerable success, or minded apparently being regarded by the world at large as Margaret Hamilton's husband. But he rather thought it was more simple than that, Roger was a damn nice chap, extremely fond of his wife, and without an ounce of envy in his makeup. 'Still,' Roger went on more confidently, 'if the situation was so bad that it was worth doing murder for I'd have heard about it.'

'Yes, I see. But you never met any of the others?'

'I was introduced to Maurice's wife, Isabel, years ago at some sort of function. I don't know that I'd even recognise her again, though I do remember thinking at the time that she was a rather superficial person. And I've heard that Julian has a girl-friend with whom he lives intermittently when his mother's away, but I've never met her.'

'What gossips you men are, darlings,' said Meg. 'Tell me about Johnny instead.'

'Wouldn't that come under the heading of gossip too?' Antony asked her, amused.

'No, because I really want what's best for him. Roger says that this Veronica Procter's sister is a much nicer sort of girl.'

'Johnny seems to think so.'

'Is he falling in love with her?'

'I sincerely hope not,' said Maitland rather forcefully, and more impulsively than was usual with him.

Meg was frowning. 'I don't understand you, darling,' she said. 'Isn't it odd about Johnny?'

'I'd say myself that he was a very ordinary young man,' said Maitland, not wishing to understand her.

'Ordinary but nice,' said Jenny.

Meg flashed her smile. 'That's just what I mean,' she said. 'Anyone would say that just to look at him. But Roger said he was really in quite a state when he arrived here last night, and why should he care if this Veronica Procter has murdered half the population of London?'

'I told you what I thought,' said Roger. 'I thought he'd taken a fancy to the sister and felt she might get hurt.'

'A girl he'd met for five minutes, or not much more?'

'I suppose there is such a thing as love at first sight,' said Roger, smiling at her, 'but I was going to add that Antony thought –'

'Mr Bellerby looks after all the criminal part of the practice,' said Antony. 'Johnny just isn't used to murder cases.'

'Then what an ordinary young man would have done,' said Meg triumphantly, 'is to rush straight here to talk to you instead of walking about for a couple of hours first. I mean he may be inexperienced, but why should that worry him when he's got you to fall back on. It isn't as if he doesn't know you very well.'

Antony had a wry look for that, but then he felt Jenny's eyes on him and turned to look at her. 'You may as well tell them, Antony,' she said. 'It isn't as if . . . after all we've always trusted Roger and Meg with all our secrets, and I know they're fond of Johnny.'

'It's really your story, love. You kept it to yourself for seven years without even telling me . . . remember?'

'Seven years, darling?' said Meg. 'You're going back to the time when he was taking Lynn Edison about.'

'Yes, that's the whole point of the story really.' He glanced again at Jenny, but she made no attempt to speak. So he launched into a very brief account of what she had told him a week ago.

'But I don't quite see,' said Meg when he had finished. 'Anyone can have a brain tumour.'

'Unfortunately, yes. But that isn't the whole story. There was espionage involved – it was before we knew you, Roger, but Meg will remember Jenny and I spending some months in Mardingley – and a series of murders, and unfortunately the whole thing came to a head in Johnny's presence. He was fifteen at the time, and it was the first occasion that his father had shown openly that his mind was affected. You can imagine the scene made rather a lasting impression on Johnny.'

'It was horrible,' said Jenny, shuddering.

'Were you there too, darling?'

63

'Yes, she was.' Antony answered for her. 'And I've never been more thankful for anything in my life, because Johnny was able to turn to her for comfort. So you see –'

'How perfectly beastly,' said Meg passionately, not waiting for him to finish. 'And in a way it was all my fault that he ever met Lynn. If he'd fallen for a different kind of girl –'

'Don't worry about it now, Meg. You knew nothing of the circumstances, and even if you had nobody could have predicted how she would react.'

'But you see, that's why Johnny doesn't like murder cases,' said Jenny.

'And now I'm sorry I asked you, dreadfully sorry.' Meg was genuinely contrite, but as usual she couldn't resist the temptation to dramatise her emotions a little. 'I remember you both going up to Mardingley that time. That was before I knew you, darling,' she added to her husband. 'And I knew something horrible must have happened there because Antony would never talk about it,' she went on, completely ignoring that fact that many things had happened to Maitland over the years that were now tacitly forbidden as topics of conversation. 'Of course I knew you always felt responsible for Johnny in some way, but I thought it must be just because you'd known his parents . . . something like that.'

'Well, as there's nothing whatever we can do about the way he feels we'd better all forget it,' said Antony. The reminder was unnecessary as he knew perfectly well, but the story had sobered the meeting, and not even Meg felt like protesting. 'Johnny realises that he can't desert Veronica Procter without hopelessly prejudicing the case against her, and he knows that I'll help him all I can. It's a nuisance, because she's a tiresome girl, but we're both in the same boat there.'

Much later, when Meg and Roger had gone and Antony and Jenny were preparing for bed, she asked him suddenly, 'You weren't surprised, were you, Antony, when you heard old Mr Keats had been murdered?'

'It explains so many things,' he told her, and for some reason he sounded apologetic.

Jenny gave him a speculative look, but she knew as well as the next woman when to leave well enough alone and did not persist in her questioning.

To her surprise, however, Antony returned to the subject later. though in an oblique fashion, when they were both in bed and the lights were turned out. 'It's a great comfort, Jenny love,' he said, 'to be married to someone who knows all your weaknesses and still doesn't seem to mind.'

Monday, April 29th

I

The next morning was sunny after a week of grey days, and it was pleasant to sit in the table by the window with coffee and the morning paper, but Antony looked up quickly when Jenny came in with some freshly made toast. 'You needn't worry about Johnny having to handle a murder case any more,' he said. 'According to this' – he tapped the copy of *The Courier* he was holding – 'our client's dead.'

'Veronica Procter? But she's quite a young woman. Was there an accident?'

'I know only what it says here.' He handed the folded newspaper across to her. 'She was found dead in the Chelsea flat at about eleven-thirty on Saturday evening. The police are investigating, so there goes our case.'

'I wonder what on earth could have happened to her. Do you suppose . . . do you suppose, Antony, she could have killed herself?'

'My dearest love, I haven't the faintest idea.' He didn't sound as if he had much interest in the question either.

'She might have thought she was going to be found out, or she might have been genuinely remorseful,' said Jenny. Antony smiled suddenly, that last, more charitable, remark was so very like his wife. 'It's all very well saying that finishes the matter,' she added. 'What will happen now about the will?'

'Veronica's heirs will scoop the pool, I suppose, unless the Keats family start another suit. Which I suppose they will,' he added thoughtfully.

'That'll be her sister, won't it? The one Johnny called Fran.'

'I've no idea what other relations Veronica may have had, or whether she'd made a will. Anyway it's none of my business.'

'Not yet,' said Jenny doubtfully.

'Well, if the sister does inherit and tries to enlist Johnny on her side I shall advise very strongly that she settle out of court,' said Antony firmly. 'After all, in the circumstances –' He retrieved the paper and scowled at it. 'If we only knew what the circumstances were,' he said.

If that was a wish it was about to be at least partially granted. The house phone rang and Jenny went to answer it on the grounds that at that hour of the day it was likely to be someone wanting her rather than wanting her husband. A moment later, however, she came back into the room with a bewildered look on her face. 'It's Inspector Sykes,' she said. 'I told Gibbs to send him up.'

'Chief Inspector,' Antony corrected her automatically, as he had been doing now for several years. 'I can't imagine . . . what in hell's name can he want with me?'

'He's working on old Mr Keats's murder, isn't he? Wouldn't it be natural for them to link Veronica Procter's death with that in some way?'

'You're becoming altogether too reasonable, love, I don't know if I can cope with it. That would be the natural thing but . . . I'd better go and let him in,' he went on, getting up. 'It's no use speculating when he'll tell us himself in a moment.'

And sure enough Sykes was stumping up the last few stairs when Antony flung his own front door open. The detective was a square-built, fresh faced man, rather heavy about the jaw, who looked far more like a farmer than a leading member of the murder squad. A farmer who had just put through a good deal at market perhaps, he had a more placid look than most men who rely on nature's favours for their living generally achieve. 'Well now, Mr Maitland, you'll forgive this early intrusion,' he said, completing his climb and coming into the hall.

'You're welcome at any time, Chief Inspector.'

'But you're wondering why I'm here.'

'I could bear to know.'

'How is – ?' But he was in the living-room by now. 'I can see for myself that all's well with you, Mrs Maitland,' he said by way of greeting to Jenny, who was a favourite of his. 'I hope the same can be said of Sir Nicholas and Lady Harding.'

'They're both very well. And they've just come back from Salzburg,' said Jenny. Sykes was always punctilious about these matters. 'There's plenty of coffee, I'll get another cup, shall I?' she added, 'And do you want to see Antony alone?'

'I don't think that's necessary and I'd hate to deprive either of us of the pleasure of your company,' Sykes assured her. 'I'm about to be indiscreet, which is why I'm alone and why I came here so early, but after we've known each other for so many years that will hardly surprise you, will it?'

Jenny laughed. 'I don't think your definition of indiscretion can tally with mine,' she told him. She disappeared kitchen-wards, and the detective turned to Antony.

'Can you spare me half an hour of your time, Mr Maitland?' he asked formally.

'As long as you like. I have a conference at eleven, that's all, and the work I'd be doing in the meantime can certainly wait. But you're arousing my curiosity, Chief Inspector. What's all this about?'

'Have you read the morning paper yet?'

'If you mean, have I seen that Veronica Procter's dead, yes it's here in a very small paragraph on the second page.'

'So the matter is finished as far as you're concerned. There's no impropriety in my asking you what opinion you've formed of the lady?'

'No harm, I suppose, but unfortunately there's nothing I can tell you. I saw her once, she wasn't altogether a likeable character, at least I didn't take to her. But I can't imagine that information is exactly useful.'

'No, I've gathered as much from other sources. But what I was really wondering about was the case of the disputed will.'

'That's something else you must have heard from other sources,' said Antony thoughtfully.

'The family's side of the case, yes. But from your client's point of view?'

'She said she'd never done anything to influence Mr Keats in her favour, nor had she maligned any of his family to him.' They had moved over to the fireside chairs by this time, Maitland taking his coffee with him, and at this point Jenny rejoined them with a clean cup and a sugar basin, knowing well that Sykes had a very sweet tooth.

'I was wondering whether the question of a settlement out of court was discussed.'

'She was against it. I think Johnny Lund had already suggested to her that he should talk to Bernard Stanley, the family's solicitor, but she wouldn't hear of it. And in one way, you know, I couldn't blame her, at that stage it didn't look as if there was much chance of the will being set aside. If Samuel Keats had formed the opinion that his family were conspiring against him in some way, even if it was a mistaken impression, it wouldn't be enough to constitute testamentary incapacity.'

'This was before – thank you, Mrs Maitland – before it was known that her patient had been poisoned?'

'Yes.'

'You'll have heard that Inspector Mayhew and I talked to her about that on Saturday afternoon.'

'Johnny Lund told me about it.'

'Was there any change in her attitude after that?'

'I didn't see her again. All I know is what Johnny told me, hearsay evidence, you should get his story yourself.'

'I shall do so, Mr Maitland. But in the meantime there can surely be no harm in your telling me what he said to you, even if it isn't something that would be accepted in evidence.'

'He said she was still adamant that she wouldn't settle.'

'A strong-minded young lady,' said Sykes thoughtfully.

'Yes, I think that's a fair enough description. I'm surprised you haven't seen Johnny yourself already, Chief Inspector.'

69

'The connection wasn't made between the two cases until some time yesterday afternoon, when I was asked to take over. Mr Lund was not at home yesterday evening.'

'I see. Well, I've answered your questions to the best of my ability, but where does the indiscretion come in?'

Sykes smiled sedately. 'I haven't come to that yet, Mr Maitland,' he said. 'Perhaps you can tell me, what will happen about the disputed will now?'

'If Miss Procter died intestate –'

'Apparently she did.'

'Then I suppose her family will inherit. She has a sister, I know.'

'Her only relative, so she tells me.'

'Is she? Then it will be up to the Keats family to recommence the action, and this time it's anybody's guess what the result will be. Though you may be in a better position than I am to make that guess, now that you've discovered how the old man met his death.'

'Not unnaturally, the members of his family are convinced that Miss Procter poisoned him.'

'If they can convince the court of that they'll win hands down.'

'I think it's rather creepy,' said Jenny suddenly. 'In a way they'd be trying her after she was dead.'

'I was just about to come to that, love, and I hope Chief Inspector Sykes is going to satisfy my curiosity.'

'Our curiosity,' Jenny corrected him.

'Yes, that's how I should have put it. How does Veronica Procter's death change things? All we know is that she was found dead late on Saturday evening, and that the police are investigating. That surely means there was something odd about her death.'

There was a long pause. Sykes might have made up his mind to be indiscreet, but habit died hard. 'Her sister found her when she came home at about half-past eleven. She was in the bathroom, where she had evidently made her way when she began to feel ill. We had the results of the post mortem so quickly because when

70

Mayhew and I were put on the case we were able to tell the pathologist what to look for. It was arsenic again. There was a tumbler beside the chair where she usually sat, evidently the poison had been taken in a glass of gin and tonic. Also beside her was a small medicine bottle, now empty, which seems to have contained a solution of the same weed-killer that was used on her late employer. Which, by the way, was the kind habitually used by the gardener at the Wimbledon house.'

'Then –'

'It seems there had been an attempt to suggest that she had committed suicide.'

'I don't quite understand. Isn't that the most obvious answer?'

'There are a few points, Mr Maitland, none of them I may as well tell you straight away conclusive by themselves. She left no note, and though that is sometimes the case by far the majority of people in a suicidal frame of mind feel an overwhelming need to explain themselves. And there are too many motives altogether for someone to have made away with her.'

'Some members of the Keats family, if they thought she was going to win the case. But surely they'd realise her death alone wouldn't cancel the will.'

'No, but think a minute. If she committed suicide it would be considered as proof of her guilt, and as she couldn't profit by what she'd done there'd be no need for any further action.'

'Unless the new heir is equally stubborn, and convinced besides of her sister's innocence.'

'And there you have it, Mr Maitland . . . another motive. If Miss Frances Procter thought she could fight the action successfully –'

'Her own sister, her twin sister,' said Jenny, horrified.

'I'm afraid, Mrs Maitland, worse things than that have been done for the sake of money. I was about to add that she may not have realised that a person can't legally benefit from a crime they have committed. And I was going to add a third point, which to my mind is much more persuasive than either of the

71

others. The amount of arsenic Veronica Procter had taken was far in excess of a fatal dose; as a nurse she must have known that.'

'But she knew her sister was coming home,' Jenny protested. 'Perhaps she just wanted to be sure there was no chance of reviving her if she was found too soon.'

'I think it might be argued that an excessive dose might have had an opposite effect, Mrs Maitland. I don't want to go into details, but the amount of purging –'

'Yes, I see,' said Jenny quickly. She picked up her cup, which rattled in the saucer as she did so.

'So that's the line you're taking. Chief Inspector . . . murder?' said Antony. He glanced for a moment at Jenny, but she was sipping her coffee and seemed to have regained her poise. 'It's interesting, because having met Miss Procter I was curious, as I told you. But although I'm grateful to you for answering my questions, I can't honestly see why you're telling me all this. It's nothing to do with me.'

'That's just the trouble, Mr Maitland, suppose it is. Suppose Frances Procter turns to Mr Lund and to you for help as her sister did.'

'I was telling Jenny before you came in, I should strongly recommend her to settle out of court.'

'That's not exactly what I meant. You see, I was talking to Chief Superintendent Briggs late last night, very much on the lines of our discussion just now. There's a lot of work to be done on the case, of course, but just at the moment he's quite convinced that Frances Procter murdered her sister. And you know when he gets an idea into his head –'

'I know that nothing in this world or the next will get it out again. But I still don't see how that concerns me.'

'Because you know as well as I do, Mr Maitland, what the Superintendent thinks of you.'

'Another of his fixed ideas. But really . . . from the sound of it you haven't had time to ask any questions yet.'

'You're right about that. At this stage the affair may go in any direction, I just can't foresee. All I'm saying, Mr Maitland, all

I'm warning you, is that if Mr Lund takes on this girl as a client he'd better find another counsel for her.'

'Come now, Sykes,' – Antony's tone endeavoured to bring a little lightness into the conversation – 'what this amounts to is telling me to give up criminal practice. I've no earthly reason to suppose that Frances Procter will either need my help or ask for it, but I'm certainly not going to do that.'

'I've got to know you pretty well over the years,' said Sykes in a ruminative manner, 'and though I felt it my duty to warn you I think I knew before I started that I was beaten. But don't you see, this case has become something special in the Superintendent's eyes? Mayhew and I were working on Samuel Keats's murder –'

'And when Briggs knew that the chief suspect was my client in another matter he immediately assumed that something funny was going on. I'm sorry I've been so slow in seeing what you were getting at, Chief Inspector. I'm not at my brightest at this time of the morning.'

'You've never taken the Superintendent's animosity towards you as seriously as I'd like you to,' said Sykes. 'You've put yourself in a vulnerable position before now, not once, but many times, and this is a case where his suspicions are already aroused. I'm telling you, Mr Maitland –'

'And I'm telling you, Chief Inspector,' Antony interrupted without ceremony, 'I see no reason why I should be involved in any way.'

'You're a friend of Mr Lund, aren't you? And he's not over-experienced in criminal matters as I understand it. If the girl has never had any need of a solicitor, it's very likely she'll turn to him.'

'Yes, but look here, supposing she does and supposing I take the case . . . you know and I know that I shan't do anything to break the law, so what is there to worry about?'

'I admit I'd rather see you out of it altogether,' said Sykes, 'but I suppose there'd not be too much harm done if only you wouldn't start your own investigation. That's where the trouble

73

comes in. You'll agree with me, Mrs Maitland?'

Jenny, who had long since made a vow to herself never to interfere in anything her husband thought to be his duty, smiled faintly and shook her head. 'I think Antony must make his own mind up about that,' she said. 'And perhaps, as he says, the question won't arise. But that doesn't mean that either of us are any the less grateful for your warning.'

'Very well.' Sykes was disappointed but not surprised. 'We must just hope that all the evidence will point in another direction, or that the case against Miss Frances Procter will be so obvious that you won't be tempted to interfere.' He picked up his cup and began to stir his coffee industriously, making sure that the five lumps of sugar that he had added to it were quite dissolved. 'I'll just drink this and then I'll be on my way,' he said. 'I know you don't see things as I do, Mr Maitland, but I thought I must speak to you now. Before we were perhaps involved on different sides of the matter, and unable to communicate until it got to court.'

'Like Jenny, I'm obliged to you,' Antony said. 'But I do decline to start worrying at this stage about something that may never happen.'

'Well, we shall see.' Sykes heaved himself out of his chair. 'Thank you, Mrs Maitland. Perhaps after all I should have asked you to leave us alone together, but if I'm any judge,' he smiled from one of them to the other, 'you'd have got it out of your husband as soon as I'd gone.' He started to move towards the door. 'Don't bother about coming with me, Mr Maitland. I know my own way out by this time.'

When he had gone Antony looked at Jenny rather helplessly. 'Does anything strike you as particularly odd about this affair?' he demanded.

'He only meant to be kind,' said Jenny.

'I know that, you don't need to remind me of it, love. I meant the amount of indiscretion there is floating about. First Geoffrey, and now Sykes. The next thing will be an angel with a flaming sword standing in my path.'

Jenny smiled at that. 'You don't think it might be a good idea to

74

take his advice,' she said rather hesitantly.

'Not you too, love! I can see why he wanted to talk to me now, while he could do so without prejudice as it were. But the occasion may never arise for me either to take his advice or ignore it.'

'There are plenty of other barristers,' Jenny pointed out.

'So there are, but none of them know Johnny's particular problems.' He saw Jenny's frown and added with something as near to impatience in his tone as ever he used to her, 'You saw how upset he was over Samuel Keats's murder, when it was obvious that would affect the case about the will in some way. If the worst comes to the worst, if this girl Fran does appeal to him for help, there's no way on earth I can let Johnny down.'

'No, I can see that and I wouldn't want you to. You'll have to think what to say to Uncle Nick,' she added, 'when Gibbs tells him Inspector Sykes has been here. You know how he always carries on about your getting involved with the police.'

Antony glanced at his watch. 'He must have left by now, I believe he's in court today. And if I avoid Astroff's at lunch time . . . you know, love, I think we ought to know by tonight whether Johnny and I are going to be called on. If Briggs is on the warpath about this unfortunate girl, Fran, she'll be among the first to be interviewed. I suppose she would be anyway, being the one to find the body, even though the local chaps must have taken a statement from her. Come to think of it, it's a bit odd Sykes didn't tell us what she had to say for herself.'

'I think he's quite convinced you'll know that soon enough,' said Jenny. 'Anyway, Antony, if the day passes without anything happening you'll be in a good position to pacify Uncle Nick tonight.'

II

The day however was not destined to pass without incident, and Detective Chief Inspector Sykes proved to be a true prophet. At a little after noon Maitland escorted to the door of chambers his solicitor and lay clients (Paul Collingwood and an amiable burglar whom he had represented several times before) and when he turned back towards his own room he found Willett hovering in the door of the clerks' office. 'Mr Lund is here to see you, Mr Maitland,' he said, 'I put him in the waiting-room.' He came closer and lowered his voice. 'I really think you should see him right away, he doesn't look at all the thing.'

'All right, Willett, thanks for the tip. Sir Nicholas isn't back, is he?'

'No, and I don't think there's much chance that even one day will see him through with this case,' said Willett. He preceded Antony to the door of the waiting-room, flung it open and said encouragingly, 'Here's Mr Maitland now, Mr Lund.'

At a quick glance, Johnny Lund seemed calm enough, but there was a haggardness about him that Maitland didn't remember having noticed before. 'We may as well go into Uncle Nick's room, Johnny,' he said. 'He'll be out all day and it's much more comfortable than mine.' But what was in his mind was that there was a small cupboard, seldom opened except for close friends or for medicinal purposes if a client of the female sex was suddenly taken faint. Johnny looked as if he could do with a stiff whisky, and come to think of it he didn't feel that one would be unwelcome himself.

So he led the way, talking as he went. 'I'm sorry to have kept you, but that was a very old client of mine. Actually, he's not so old himself, but I've acted for his father too, and if I were old enough I gather I might have been acting for his grandfather and great-grandfather and so on *ad infinitum*. I've tried once or twice to get him on the right track, he's an intelligent fellow, but he's a great believer in tradition and any other occupation than house-breaking would seem *infra dig* to him. Or *infra dignitatem*, as I've no doubt Uncle Nick would prefer me to say.' He was in the room now and waited for Johnny to pass him before he closed the door. 'Go and sit down over there,' he gesticulated towards the one easy chair near the fireplace, 'and I'll make free with Uncle

76

Nick's desk in his absence. I think a drink would do us both good, don't you?'

So far Johnny hadn't spoken a word, but he crossed the room obediently and seated himself. He did murmur his thanks when Antony put a glass into his hand, but he waited until the other man was seated before he looked directly at him and said abruptly, 'You know what's happened to Veronica Procter?'

'I saw the paper this morning.' Antony was sipping his drink, hoping that his example would prompt Johnny to sample his also.

'I hope it was suicide, though I've got to say she didn't look as if she'd anything like that in mind when I left them on Saturday. But now there's Fran Procter telling me the police are treating it as a case of murder, and they want to see her this afternoon. I told her Mr Bellerby dealt with . . . that kind of thing, but she said she knew me and would feel more at ease and it was only a matter of being there. Veronica had said that it was important to have someone if the police were asking questions. Only it's a murder case, Antony, I don't honestly think I can cope.'

'You coped well enough when Lynn Edison was accused of murder,' Antony reminded him.

'That was different.'

'Drink your scotch, Johnny, and then tell me exactly what the difference was.'

Johnny Lund looked down at the glass in his hand as though he had never seen it before, then he took a quick swig and put it down with a thump on the table at his elbow. 'It had simply never occurred to me then that I was . . . not quite like everyone else. Even Jenny accepted me, as you did, even though you knew all there was to know about Dad. And Sir Nicholas too, though of course you must have told him, and Mr Bellerby. I didn't even think of saying anything about it when you got him to give me my articles, but naturally I did when he offered me a partnership and it didn't make any difference to him at all.'

'How many times do I have to tell you, Johnny, there's no reason why it should.'

'That's what I thought, until Lynn said . . . I don't want to talk

77

about it, but it made me see how wrong I'd been not realising I was different. Well, I was committed to Veronica Procter before any question of murder came up so though I didn't like it I could hardly back out. But now there's this perfectly nice girl wanting my help. It may only be to sit in at one interview as she says and that'll be the end, but supposing it isn't. I'll have committed myself again.'

'All right, supposing you have. This afternoon will be plain sailing, no worse than the interview you sat in on Saturday with the sister. And if the worst comes to the worst you're perfectly competent to draw up a brief, even if it is a rather more serious matter than you're used to dealing with.'

'Not without your help. Will you help me, Antony?'

'Most of the solicitors for whom I work claim I take too much on my own shoulders,' said Maitland, smiling.

'But that's just what I want.'

'Lynn's defection upset you a good deal, didn't it?'

'Yes, it did, because it made me see that I'd been taking an awful lot for granted in my relationships with other people. Didn't Jenny tell you?'

'Not until the other day.' He paused, considering. He could hardly let Johnny down, he'd always felt a certain responsibility for him; on the other hand if Briggs had got the bit between his teeth over this one, having him for her counsel might not do Fran Procter any good. But somehow or other that could be got around, his first duty was to Johnny, and at that moment the thought of Sykes's warning of the possible consequences to himself never entered his head. 'We'll work together if it becomes necessary,' he promised. 'But, you know, we can discuss this much better after you've heard what your new client has to say.'

'Well, I thought –' Johnny suddenly remembered his scotch and finished it before he went on. 'I know it's an awful imposition, Antony, but if you have time could you come with me this afternoon?'

'It's hardly usual.'

'She won't know.'

'No, but –' He caught himself up on the point of mentioning Sykes's name. 'The detectives who are doing the interviewing are certain to know me,' he said.

'Does that matter?'

'It may raise a few eyebrows.'

'What if it does? Honestly, Antony, I don't think I can get through it on my own.'

'Tell me, Johnny, does all this mean that you have reason to expect that Miss Procter will be charged?'

'No, but . . . you can think up a good reason for being there,' he said more confidently.

'So I might, but at this stage it really isn't necessary –' He allowed the sentence to trail into silence and Johnny pounced triumphantly on the slight hesitation in his voice.

'I knew you'd agree,' he said. 'Besides, you know, I'd like you to meet Fran Procter. She may look like Veronica, but she isn't a bit like her inside.'

'What time is this confrontation to take place?'

'About two o'clock, at the Chelsea flat where I was before.'

'Then we'd better get a quick lunch and get out there immediately. Or perhaps the other way round, if we go to Chelsea first we're certain to be able to find somewhere to eat.'

'I don't feel a bit hungry,' said Johnny. But when it came to the point it was Maitland who, against all precedent, left most of what was on his plate, while Johnny easily made a clean sweep of everything that was set before him.

III

The Chelsea flat was larger than Maitland had expected. In fact it wasn't really a flat at all, occupying the two top floors of an old house in a narrow alleyway in the crowded area between Chelsea

Embankment and the King's Road. The girl who admitted them was certainly exactly like their former client, which startled Antony rather even though he had been expecting it. She had been crying, he thought, or perhaps the redness of her eyes was due to a sleepless night. Either way she accepted his presence and Johnny's rather incoherent explanation of it calmly, saying rather apologetically as she led the way into a tiny sitting-room, 'I suppose I'm being silly about this, but Veronica was the sensible one, you know, and she said it would be very foolish ever to talk to the police without legal representation. She said they could twist what you said and make it sound quite different, and I don't know anything about the law and I suppose when they said they were coming I rather lost my head.'

As Johnny seemed temporarily to have been struck dumb, Antony thought he'd better take up the running. 'The law's a mystery to most people,' he said comfortingly, 'except to those of us who choose to make our living by it.' He looked round the room appreciatively. 'You've got a very attractive place here,' he said, 'and what's more it looks very comfortable.'

'Oh dear, I should have been asking you to sit down.' That wasn't what Antony had meant at all but he obeyed her gesture and took a chair near the window. 'On this floor,' Fran went on, 'it's just bedroom and sitting-room and the usual offices – well I'm lucky really, the kitchen's quite big enough to eat in – and upstairs I have my studio.'

'Are you an artist, then?'

'Trying to be. I do have a job that keeps the wolf from the door, and I've sold a few things. But it takes time to get established, and I don't really know if I'm good enough.'

'I wonder if you know Clare Canning.'

'Oh yes, of course I do, but she's a lot better than I am. Anyway it's Clare Charlton now.'

'Yes, I know.'

'Don't tell me you're *that* Mr Maitland, the one Clare talks about.'

'I'm afraid I am.'

80

'Does that mean . . . Mr Lund, are things worse than I thought?'

'It's just,' said Johnny, finding his voice, 'that I'm completely inexperienced in this kind of thing, and as Mr Maitland is an old friend of mine –' He broke off there and smiled at her. 'I really don't think you've anything to worry about,' he said.

'It would be interesting to know, however,' Maitland put in, 'exactly what Miss Procter's own estimate of the situation is.'

'You must think I'm a perfectly horrid person,' said Fran. 'I ought to be sitting here with a wet handkerchief dabbing my eyes and sniffing occasionlly. And I'm terribly, terribly sorry that Veronica is dead; we'd nothing in common except that people say we looked alike, but when your memories go back to the nursery there's always a bond. When I found her . . . it was such a shock I don't think I took it in until the next day and then I cried and cried. But it's no use pretending I'll miss her terribly because I shan't.'

'Thank you for being so frank with us. You were going to tell us what you thought when you found your sister dead.'

Before she could answer the doorbell sounded again and she went out with a brief apology to answer it, coming back in a few moments later with Detective Chief Inspector Sykes and Detective Inspector Mayhew in tow.

Sykes gave Maitland what could only be described as a speaking glance but made no comment on his presence. Mayhew, however, a dark, tall, rather silent man who generally prefaced each of his remarks by a rather rumbling sound which always reminded Antony of a grandfather clock getting ready to strike, said bluntly, 'I'm surprised to find you here, Mr Maitland.'

Antony looked from one of the detectives to the other. 'You remember Clare Canning, who is now Clare Charlton,' he said, and did not wait for a reply because he knew it must be in the affirmative. 'Miss Procter's a friend of hers, and that's my only excuse for being here.'

'Quite a cosy little party,' said Sykes rather grumpily. 'Mr Lund is an old friend of yours, and Miss Procter is a friend of a friend.' Maitland met his glance blandly, but he couldn't help feeling that things were getting unnecessarily complicated. He carefully avoided meeting Fran Procter's eyes. 'If we all sit down we can get on with the business at hand,' he suggested. 'Which is your favourite chair, Miss Procter? I promise I won't interrupt.'

'Unless you think it's necessary,' said Mayhew rather dryly.

'Well, yes, unless I think it's necessary,' Antony agreed. 'I may have said this to you before, Inspector Mayhew, I've certainly said it to the Chief Inspector here, but if you were a strong swimmer and saw a friend in difficulty you wouldn't hesitate about giving him or her a helping hand.'

By the time they were all seated the little room seemed to have grown again, five people standing about in it were more than it could be expected to accommodate. 'I'm sorry, Miss Procter,' said Sykes, 'to make you go over all this again when I know you gave a statement to the local police, but I'm sure you'll understand there may be questions to be answered that they didn't think to ask. It was only when a possible connection between Mr Samuel Keats's death and your sister's was recognised that Inspector Mayhew and I came into the matter.'

'Yes, I think I understand that,' she said quietly. 'You think Veronica killed him because of the will, only I'm quite sure she'd never have done a thing like that.'

If Geoffrey Horton had been there he and Maitland would probably have exchanged despairing glances at that point, being all too familiar with witnesses who couldn't believe that any of their friends or relations were capable of villainy. As it was Antony held his peace. 'Just at the moment that doesn't concern us, Miss Procter,' Sykes told her. 'But we should like a first-hand account of what happened on Saturday evening.'

'You were here yourselves until six o'clock.'

'About that. How long did Mr Lund stay after we left?'

'Five . . . ten minutes. I don't know really but it wasn't very long.'

She glanced at Johnny who said stolidly, 'Not more than five minutes, I should think.'

'Yes, you're probably right.' She turned back to Sykes again. 'When I went down with him to the front door we talked there for a few minutes, and when I came back into this room again Veronica was already on the phone. I don't know who she was talking to, but she was saying that she must see them as soon as possible. I was going to go out to the kitchen in case it was a private call, but before I could do so she said, "Yes, that'll do," and put the receiver down. When she turned from the phone and saw me she said, 'He's coming at nine o'clock. Couldn't you go to a film or something?' I'd meant to stay home that evening but I thought . . . I suppose all my life I've been used to doing what Veronica wanted, she was a much stronger personality than I am, so I looked at the paper and went to the second house at the Paris cinema to see a French film called *The Tall Blond Man with One Black Shoe*.'

'Can you tell us what it was about, Miss Procter?'

'One moment.' Maitland had been looking out of the window, as though unconcerned with the proceedings, but now he turned quickly. 'As I understand it, Chief Inspector, this was to be a very informal interview, because you very naturally wished to hear for yourself what Miss Procter had to say about what must have been a very unpleasant experience for her.'

'You're quite right, Mr Maitland. Obviously it hasn't escaped your attention that we gave no warning to Miss Procter, which in certain circumstances we should have been obliged to do, even in the face of so much legal talent.'

'Don't you think your last question, that she should describe the film she saw, has certain implications?'

'I'll forgo it if you like, but you won't like my next question either,' Sykes told him bluntly.

'In any case,' said Fran, 'I don't mind in the least telling you what it was about. The man in the title was a musician, and his friends in the same orchestra had played a trick on him, so that he had to return from an engagement in another town wearing one black and one brown shoe. Some intelligence agents had been sent to meet the plane, not knowing the man they were supposed

83

to follow by sight, and this oddity led them to think that the musician was the man they were looking for. It led to all kinds of complications, they kept putting in reports of his activities which were perfectly innocent, of course, but they interpreted the most simple actions as something sinister. As a matter of fact it was one of the funniest things I've ever seen only . . . I don't really like to think about it now, because if I hadn't gone out – '

'And you went to the cinema alone?' Sykes persisted. 'You didn't ring up a friend, for instance, and ask them to accompany you?'

'No.' She glanced at Johnny and then at Maitland, who gave her a slight nod. Obviously the girl had seen the film, but he suspected that the detectives' next job would be to make inquiries among her friends as to whether they had any knowledge of her viewing it previously. 'At such short notice it didn't seem worth while,' Fran was saying. 'Though if you're going to ask me next,' she added rather defiantly, 'whether I saw anybody I knew, or whether the people at the cinema know me, the answer's No to both those questions.'

'You mustn't take my inquiries personally, Miss Procter. As Mr Maitland said they're of a preliminary nature only, and there will be a lot more questions asked of a great many more people before we are finished. So you went to the cinema because your sister was expecting a visitor, a man, we must assume, from her use of the word "he".'

'Which reminds me, Chief Inspector,' said Maitland. 'The investigations which your local colleagues made . . . I presume they interviewed the people on the ground floor first, as well as the occupants of the other houses in the street, to see if anyone had noticed a man coming here about nine o'clock that evening.'

'Certainly that was done, and the inquiries are still continuing because, of course, not everyone was home when our men called. So far nothing pertinent has been discovered.'

'Thank you, Chief Inspector.' They were coming to the crux of the matter now, and there was something vulnerable about Fran Procter that made him want to soften its impact on her. 'I think,' he said, turning to her, 'that these gentlemen would like to know whether you can make a guess at the identity of the man your sister was expecting.'

If Sykes resented this taking over of his task he made no sign, nor did he remind Maitland of his promise not to interfere. 'That would be very helpful,' he agreed.

'But I don't know,' said Fran, almost despairingly. 'Veronica was living here for about three weeks, ever since old Mr Keats died. And when she stayed with me before between jobs she was always out a lot, but she never asked anyone here. This time was different, she hardly went out at all except to do some shopping until about a week ago. Since then she's been out on two evenings as far as I remember, but she never said who she was going to meet.'

'A not-so-communicative young lady?'

'I suppose not.'

Inspector Mayhew's characteristic rumble announced his intention of joining in the conversation. 'I've been told you were twins,' he said, so that Maitland thought he must have seen that for himself if he'd viewed the body, and could only be thankful that the detective had too much tact to say so.

'I suppose you're thinking that means we should have been very close,' said Fran. 'I know I've heard extraordinary stories about twins who were brought up separately, and when they came together years later they found their lives had followed very similar patterns. Well, physically I think that was true about Veronica and me, when we were children we always went down together with the same ailments, which must have been convenient for mother, but I suppose that doesn't mean much with infectious things because they usually go through the whole family anyway. But we had our appendixes out within a week of each other, and when Veronica sprained her ankle in gym class at school, I had a fall a couple of days later and did exactly the same thing.'

'That raises an interesting question,' said Sykes, 'and this is pure curiosity, Mr Maitland, I realise it is nothing to do with why we're here. When you were apart from your sister did you have any knowledge of how she was feeling? Whether she was sick or unhappy, for instance?'

'No, I'm afraid not. I think I'm glad about that, though it might have spared me the shock I got when I came in and found her. I mean if you carry that question of yours to its logical conclusion I'd surely have known she was dead.'

'I suppose so. But you were going to tell us, I think, that these physical similarities of yours didn't extend to – to your characters.'

'Yes, I was.'

'Which was the elder, by the way?'

'Veronica, by thirty-five minutes I've been told. Do you think that could explain why she was a much stronger character, when we were children I always did what she wanted, just as I did the other night? Then she took up nursing, which I'm afraid I couldn't possibly have done.'

'Did that surprise you?'

'In a way, a little. She hated the training I think, but once she'd made up her mind to a thing she'd go through with it.'

'There's one more question I must put to you, but I think I'll ask Mr Lund to answer it first. After Inspector Mayhew and I left here on Saturday what sort of a frame of mind was Miss Procter in? Had our talk upset her badly?'

'I didn't know her well, Chief Inspector,' said Johnny, 'but I should say she was more indignant than anything else.'

'Can you add anything to that, Miss Procter? You must have been here together for some time before you went out.'

'Yes, I think indignant is a very good word for the way she felt.' She smiled suddenly from Sykes to Mayhew and then looked back at the Chief Inspector again. 'She wasn't very complimentary about either of you,' she told them.

'That doesn't really surprise me,' said Sykes good-humouredly. 'But – think back carefully, Miss Procter – was there anything at all in her manner to suggest that she might be considering taking her own life?'

86

'No and . . . I have to say this Chief Inspector even in spite of what I thought for a moment later on. I can't imagine any circumstances in which Veronica would have done that.'

'Then I'm afraid we must come to the difficult part of your story.'

'My coming home and finding her?' There was a distinct quaver in Fran's voice now. 'This room, where I expected to find her, was empty and there was no sign that anything was wrong. She must have got to the bathroom where I found her before – before the sickness started.'

'What did you think when you saw what had happened?'

'Just that she'd been taken suddenly ill. I think I was too shocked by what I saw to be really surprised, and I rushed back into this room to telephone the doctor. I was fairly sure she was dead but I might have been wrong, but then I saw the glass on the table by the chair she usually used, and that wasn't surprising because she often had a gin and tonic in the evening. But there was that little bottle beside it, and I'd never seen that before, and it made me wonder whether she had been more upset than I realised, and had taken something. It was only then that I thought about the man who was coming, and surely he'd had a drink with her, and where was his glass? So I phoned the doctor immediately and he said he'd be round right away, but I should call the hospital to send an ambulance as well in case there was anything to be done for her. There are lots of them around here, you know, St Walburga's where she trained is the nearest, but the doctor said when he saw Veronica that the police must be informed, so I might have saved them the journey. I don't know whether he suspected something right away, or whether it was just that she hadn't been his patient, so he couldn't sign the death certificate. But before he came I'd been to look in the kitchen, and I found a glass that had obviously been washed up and left to drain.'

'Might not your sister have done that after her visitor had gone?'

'No, not unless she'd changed her normal habits completely.

87

She had a thing about washing-up, couldn't bear anything to be left lying around, and she wouldn't leave them on the draining board either, they had to be dried and put away immediately.'

'I think,' said Antony, 'that perhaps at this point, Chief Inspector, you should tell Miss Procter exactly what the doctor said about the cause of death, and the time during which the poison was taken.'

Sykes gave him a look that said as clearly as if he had spoken, 'You mean you'd like to know.' But he added aloud, obligingly enough, 'I'm afraid there's no doubt that the cause of your sister's death was poisoning by arsenic –'

'Like Mr Keats!' exclaimed Fran, and clapped her hand over her mouth as though what she had said was an indiscretion.

'– that the poison was contained in the same week-killer that caused her employer's death, which had been brought here in the medicine bottle you mentioned and mixed in her glass of gin and tonic. I'm afraid I can be less specific as to the time during which it must have been administered –'

'Whether self-administered or not,' Antony interrupted.

'– but the doctors are of the opinion that she might have taken it any time between eight and ten o'clock. I don't want to distress you with further details, Miss Procter, but she had taken a massive dose. The effects vary from one person to another, but this was far more than has ever been known to be fatal.'

'But Veronica would never –' Fran began.

'There's also the question of fingerprints,' Maitland interrupted her.

'None were found except yours and your sister's,' said Sykes, rather pointedly directing his answer to Fran. 'You're obviously an extremely careful housekeeper.'

'That was Veronica, I expect, not me. I daresay it was her nurse's training that made her so very particular.'

'Nothing on the medicine bottle?' Antony inquired.

'No prints of any kind, it had obviously been wiped clean.' And that's another of your reasons, thought Maitland to himself, for thinking it was murder, and a more cogent reason than any of the others you quoted to me. If Veronica had killed herself she'd have had no reason to do that particular bit of cleaning up.'

Fran had obviously also taken the point. 'I told you she wouldn't have killed herself,' she said, too quickly this time for Maitland to stop her.

The two detectives left soon after that. 'Thank you,' said Fran, coming back into the room after seeing them out. 'I'm awfully glad you were here . . . both of you.'

'I don't think I was much help,' said Johnny despondently.

'That's nonsense and you know it. You could have managed perfectly well alone,' Antony told him. 'You see, Miss Procter, all my friends tell me I talk too much, and when they know me as well as Johnny does they're inclined to let me get on with it.'

'You didn't want me to say that Veronica wouldn't have committed suicide,' said Fran. 'I saw your expression when I came out with it just now. But it's perfectly obvious this man that was coming must have brought the arsenic with him, I'd never seen the bottle before and I'm sure I should have done. Unless she'd hidden it away very carefully,' she added frowning a little over the thought, 'but, no, I just don't believe that. Somebody killed her, I don't know who but somebody.'

'It would be rather a coincidence, wouldn't it, if her death was unrelated to that of her recent employer?'

'Yes, I suppose it would.' She thought about that for a moment. 'Are you trying to tell me, Mr Maitland, that perhaps one of Mr Keats's family killed her, so that she couldn't inherit from him?'

'It wouldn't have helped,' said Johnny. 'Unless the will is set aside your sister inherits and you inherit from her.'

'But that's a horrible idea! I couldn't possibly take their money.'

'Did your sister know that's how you felt?'

'Oh yes, I told her that right out. I'm afraid we had a quarrel about it, but it wasn't any use trying to influence Veronica so after that I just kept quiet. But then on Saturday, after you'd gone, Mr Lund, I mentioned it again. It did seem to me with Mr

89

Keats being poisoned . . . well it wasn't a very nice situation, was it? But she just told me not to be a little fool, everything would be all right. That was while we were having dinner before I went out.'

'So if you don't mean to accept the legacy the case to have the will set aside will go through unopposed,' said Antony.

'As far as I'm concerned, yes. But I don't know if Veronica left a will.'

'The police must have searched this flat, did they find one?' Sykes's visit that morning had left him in the awkward position of having to remember how much or how little he was supposed to know.

'If they did they didn't tell me.'

'That's one thing they would have done, I'm sure, it would have been most improper not to. And she came to your firm, Johnny, saying she'd never had any dealings with a solicitor. Wasn't that what you told me?'

'That's right, I remember quite clearly.'

'And all her belongings are here now?'

'Yes. There are two trunks up in the studio, she just unpacked what she needed, but I know the police went through them.'

'So it looks as if you're the one to make the decision, Miss Procter, if the family decide to go ahead with the case, that is.'

'I've already made it. Obviously the money should go to them.'

'A settlement out of court might be arranged from which you would benefit . . . only slightly if that's the way you want it,' he added, seeing her look of revulsion.

'No, it wouldn't be fair. But none of them could have known how I felt, so that takes away their motive, doesn't it?'

'Perhaps that's something only Veronica could have told us. There must be some connection, only we're too blind to see it at the moment. Do I understand the position correctly, you have no other relatives?'

'There were just the two of us.' He waited in silence, and after a moment she went on. 'We were brought up in the country, but

90

when Veronica came to St Walburga's to do her training, mother thought it was a good opportunity for me to come too as I wanted to go to an art school. Since then both our parents have died.'

'But you must have some friends from the old days.'

'I'm afraid there's nobody we've kept in close touch with. There are some school friends I still write to, but I think Veronica was glad to break all her ties. She didn't like country life. Said it made people dull.'

'And more recently?'

'If you mean Veronica's friends, I just don't know. Of course, I met some of the girls she trained with, but since she was doing private work I've really seen very little of her, and even when I did . . . she was never one for talking much about her own affairs.'

'Then if she didn't kill herself – and the police as well as you, Miss Procter, seem to have made up their minds that she didn't –' He broke off there, but a small cold voice added in his mind, "And if you, my girl, are telling us the truth." But not unnaturally he didn't say that aloud.

'The Keats family don't seem to have known about the new will,' said Johnny. 'Supposing one of them was in urgent need of money and killed the old man to get it, what do you think he'd have felt like when he knew someone else was going to scoop the pool? That might be a sufficient motive . . . revenge.'

'But that's a marvellous idea . . . really clever,' said Fran. 'That must be what happened, mustn't it, Mr Maitland?'

'There are, I suppose, as many different motives for murder as there are murderers,' said Antony, and smiled at her. 'Yes, it's certainly a possibility.'

Fran chose to take this as an enthusiastic endorsement of Johnny's theory. 'I knew Veronica didn't kill anybody,' she said, 'any more than she'd have killed herself. So all we have to do is find out who really did it.'

'All we have to do,' echoed Maitland warily. 'It's up to the police, Miss Procter.'

'Well, I must say they were very nice, both times they came here, not a bit what I would have expected, but to anyone who didn't know her it would stick out a mile that Veronica had poisoned Mr Keats. I don't blame them for thinking that, but I can't say it's an idea that I'd want to get about.'

'Slow up a bit. What exactly are you suggesting?'

'Well, I thought perhaps . . . Mr Maitland, Clare says you've helped ever so many people find out the truth about things like this, and after all Mr Lund is my solicitor now and he's been very kind and helpful. So I wondered . . . I know you're both very busy men, but if you could find out who really killed Mr Keats, we could do what you said and have a settlement out of court and I'd keep just enough to pay your fees and they could have the rest. Except for the one that did the murder, of course.'

Antony did his best to keep the amusement that was welling up inside him out of his voice as he replied. 'I'm afraid that's not a very practical suggestion, Miss Procter. You remember what I told Chief Inspector Sykes, I came here as a friend.'

'Well, I'm glad you feel that way, but that wasn't what Mr Lund said. He said it was because you'd had more experience in these things than he has.'

'That's true but once I realised you knew Clare, that seemed the easiest explanation of my presence,' Maitland told her. 'But as a friend, if I try to help you in this way there'll certainly be no question of payment. While as for Mr Lund, I don't think he'd feel it ethical either to charge a fee when there's so slim a chance of success. After all, we have none of the facilities the police have at their disposal. You mustn't expect too much of us.'

'But will you try?'

'If you really want me to.' He saw Johnny's startled expression, but gave him a look that silenced any protest he might have been about to make. 'But only if you promise not to be disappointed if nothing comes of it.' (If this absurd child was thinking of him as a sort of private detective the sooner she got that out of her head the better.) 'And only on the terms I mentioned.'

92

'As a friend,' she said. 'In that case I think you'd better call me Fran. And you too, of course,' she added turning to Johnny. 'It's very kind of you both.'

'As a matter of fact,' said Antony, as though the idea had only just occurred to him, 'I think it would probably be better if I did my poking about alone. People will so often talk much more freely to one person than they would two. Then I'll make my report to Mr Lund as your solicitor, and he can pass it on to you.'

'That will be splendid, but I hope I shall see you again, Mr Maitland.' Both men were on their feet now and she gave her hand solemnly to each in turn. 'You see, I just don't think the police are working along the right lines,' she said seriously. 'And after all it's only fair to Veronica as well. I know she was sharp with people sometimes, and some people didn't like her because of that, but she was a nurse after all and nurses don't kill people.'

IV

When Maitland arrived home that evening Sir Nicholas had got back from court before him and the study door was standing invitingly open. It didn't need Gibbs's intervention, 'Sir Nicholas would like a word with you, Mr Maitland,' to turn his steps in that direction. Jenny was there and he bent to kiss her as soon as he had greeted the others.

'Help yourself to sherry, my dear boy,' said Sir Nicholas with a cordiality that his nephew immediately suspected.

'Thank you, Uncle Nick, I will. Does anyone need a refill?'

'For the moment I think not,' said Sir Nicholas, and waited until the pale straw-coloured liquid was actually being poured before adding, 'And then you can tell us all about the visit Chief Inspector Sykes paid here this morning.'

It shouldn't have startled him, he'd known what was coming, but his hand wavered a little and a few drops of the sherry were spilled. 'Gibbs told you, I suppose,' said Antony mopping them up with his handkerchief, 'and I see you kidnapped Jenny to assure my attendance.' He turned then with the glass in his hand and took a sip, since it was over-full, before he crossed the room. 'Hasn't she told you?'

'Haven't asked her,' said Vera. The reason for which was obvious really, they all knew Jenny's explanations of old.

'Oh, it was just Sykes playing the mother-hen again. A sort of gipsy's warning about getting involved in the affairs of Fran Procter now that her sister's dead. You saw that in the paper this morning, I suppose,' he added.

'Yes, I did, and the account was amplified a little this evening. The police are treating it as a case of murder,' said Sir Nicholas, obviously quoting, 'but it seems rather quick work if they've already made up their minds that the sister is guilty.'

'I suppose I'd better tell you the whole thing,' said Antony in a resigned tone. 'Sykes hasn't made up his mind, he's barely got started, but as soon as Briggs heard that the dead girl had been a client of mine in the matter of the will he immediately suspected some funny business. Well, you know what he's like, Uncle Nick, he doesn't need a reason for thinking the worst of me. I don't quite know by what process he decided that she'd been poisoned by her sister, but I daresay it was at least half way reasonable to think that in any dealings with the police Fran Procter would call on Johnny, as her sister had done, and that Johnny would call on me. So Sykes thought he'd talk to me while he still could, before there was any question of involvement. Which was kind of him, I think.' He set down his glass carefully and seated himself beside his wife on the sofa.

'Very kind,' said Sir Nicholas. 'Now, if you can tell me also that you have taken his advice –'

'Not exactly, sir. The police wanted to see Fran Procter this afternoon, and she appealed to Johnny, knowing no other member of the legal profession, and Johnny appealed to me. I sat in on the session.'

'I might have known it! Surely even you, Antony, can see that the police would think that a little odd.'

'You're always complaining that people think I'm unortho-
dox, so I might as well live up to my reputation,' said Maitland
rather impatiently. 'In any case a very good excuse came to hand,
it turns out she's a friend of Clare's, so what could I do but try to
help her?'

'And what was the outcome of this interview?'

'She gave an account of what happened on Saturday evening
after Sykes and Mayhew left, having interviewed her sister
Veronica.' He gave them the facts briefly.

'And you believed her?' asked Sir Nicholas.

'I wasn't sure at first, but I think now that I do.'

'The question is, what would be her motive?' said Vera.

'The same as Veronica's for killing the old man . . . money,'
said Antony. 'She says she wouldn't take a penny anyway, it's
only right the family should inherit.'

'Might be being clever.' That was Vera again.

'That's very true. And the fact that she wants me to prove that
Veronica wasn't a murderess might add to its likelihood.'

Sir Nicholas sat up suddenly very straight in his chair. '*What*
did you say?' he inquired awfully.

Antony repeated his statement, adding Fran's ingenious offer
of payment. 'I refused, of course,' he added.

'So I should hope. But did you agree to do what she wanted?'
Sir Nicholas asked suspiciously.

'Well, as a matter of fact –'

'Antony, I have put up with a great deal of foolishness from
you, but this is beyond anything. It's perfectly obvious that
Veronica Procter was guilty.'

'I had my reasons, Uncle Nick. Fran doesn't seem to realise
she's under suspicion, or doesn't take it seriously if she does. I
want to talk to the family to protect her, and this gives me an
excuse.'

'If she were a client of yours in whose innocence you
believed –'

'Don't you see, sir, she may well become one? I think anyone

95

would agree that the two deaths are connected in some way, so if Fran is innocent that only leaves the members of the Keats family. Rather a wide field, I'm afraid.'

'And what will Briggs say when you start meddling with the police inquiries?'

'I can't see that it will be any of his business. If these people see me it will be their own decision, I shan't force myself on them. And I'm pretty certain that neither Sykes nor Mayhew will say a word to him if they hear about it. You know Sykes, Uncle Nick, and Mayhew has always been extremely friendly.'

Sir Nicholas leaned back again and picked up the cigar that had been smouldering beside him. 'I think,' he said, 'we could all do with another drink. And you'd better do the honours, Antony, because my strength seems to have deserted me.'

V

Back upstairs in their own quarters Antony followed Jenny into the kitchen and hovered near the door as she took out the casserole which she had left in the oven. 'Ought I to be laying the table?' he asked without any great enthusiasm.

'No, everything's ready,' said Jenny. 'You can bring the plates if you don't mind.' For a moment after the meal was on the table she concentrated on transferring the food from the dish to their plates, while Antony went back to the refrigerator for a bottle of white wine and a couple of glasses, which he set down within easy reach of her. Even with the multiple gadgets now available for pulling corks, that was something his injured shoulder didn't allow him to do, or not without considerable discomfort, and Jenny set about the task without comment as soon as she had finished serving.

'Celebrating?' she asked.

'Hardly.' He was tired and she knew it, there was no need for

96

further explanation between them. He accepted his glass, raised it in a silent toast to her, but then stopped when it was only half way to his lips. 'Jenny love, you're not worrying about what Sykes told us this morning? I assure you I don't intend to do anything foolish.'

Jenny smiled at that, and raised her glass to him in her turn. 'Here's to my sensible husband,' she said. 'But, Antony, do you really think Veronica Procter did murder old Mr Keats?'

'It's possible that she didn't. Quite honestly, love, I haven't got as far as that myself yet.'

'Then –'

'What I *have* made up my mind about – pretty well made up my mind about,' he amended, 'is that Fran Procter didn't murder her sister. I think, however, it's very possible she may be accused of it, and if my meddling is done before that happens there's far less likelihood of Briggs taking umbrage about it.'

'Yes, I see that, and I see too that you couldn't possibly turn Johnny down when he asked for your help. By the way, does Vera know . . . why this sort of thing upsets Johnny so much, I mean?'

'She thinks he's a – a sort of legacy from one of the cases I've been involved in in the past,' said Antony. 'But Uncle Nick understands what the trouble is, thank Heaven one doesn't have to spell things out for him, and if necessary he'll tell her. I was going to say that I had another motive, Jenny, one I didn't dare mention downstairs, for taking on this rather odd assignment.'

'I want to hear, of course, but don't let your dinner get cold.'

They ate in silence for a few minutes but presently Antony's plate was empty; he pushed it a little away from him and picked up his glass. 'You see, love,' he said, 'I really think – I know they're making a joke about it, at least Meg was – but I really think Johnny may be falling in love with Fran.'

'Oh dear, I don't want him to get hurt again,' said Jenny.

'This girl wouldn't hurt him, not in the way Lynn did anyway,' said Antony.

'You sound very positive about that.'

97

'Yes I am. She's very young, in fact it's hard to believe she's the same age as her sister, even though there's absolutely no difference that I can tell in their appearance. But I think she has principles, she may not fall in love with Johnny herself but if she wants to refuse him she wouldn't do it in a cruel way. You see, love, two things may happen. The interview with Sykes and Mayhew today may have ended the matter as far as she's concerned, except that if somebody else is brought to trial for it she'll obviously have to give evidence of finding the body. If that's the case these inquiries of mine will give Johnny plenty of chance to see her again, I told her that was how we'd arrange it. On the other hand, if an arrest follows when the police have completed their inquiries . . . don't you see that would be a way Johnny could get hurt frightfully, if I'm right about his feelings that is, without her being able to help it.'

'Yes, I see that of course. What would be the prosecution's case against her?'

'You heard what Sykes said this morning about the likelihood of it being murder, not suicide. There's another reason for thinking that, the bottle that had contained the poison had been wiped clean of fingerprints.'

'But you said that a solution of the same weed-killer that was used to kill Mr Keats had been given to Veronica. How could Fran have got hold of it?'

'The stuff can be purchased anywhere. I think the prosecution would say that Fran was fully cognisant of what Veronica had done, and able to prepare herself in good time to get rid of her sister. And naturally she'd put the stuff she meant to use into an anonymous bottle, and dispose of the packet of weed-killer. Then, of course, when the police seemed to have got on to Veronica's crime the matter became urgent.'

'But it didn't,' said Jenny. 'If Veronica murdered the old man she couldn't profit by that, and consequently Fran in her turn couldn't profit from her sister's death.'

'*We* know that, love, but I wonder how many lay people do, unless they read detective stories, of course. Fran's an artist, I told you that – didn't I? – and any jury would be ready to believe that such an idea would never enter her head. And you see there's one big objection to it being anybody else but Fran. If the two deaths are unconnected it's a damned unlikely coincidence. If they are connected it boils down to one of the family, or one of the servants, or Fran. And if Veronica killed Mr Keats, which as you pointed out was by far the most likely thing to have happened, why should one of his family come along and poison her? Johnny said, perhaps revenge, but I don't buy that. There wasn't even a financial motive, because once it was known that the testator had died of poisoning within a month of making a new will there's not a court in the land who wouldn't have accepted the family's request to set the will aside and re-instate the old one.'

'But still you think Fran is innocent?'

'Jenny love, you know me. I think she is, but I'm not sure about anything. And I haven't quite finished the prosecution's case yet.'

'You'd better tell me the rest of it then.'

'It arises really from what I told you downstairs of Fran's own story. There's absolutely no proof about the telephone call she said she overheard, or Veronica's statement that "he" was coming at nine o'clock. The doctors say the poison could have been administered some time between eight and ten, which is vague enough in all conscience, but it means that Fran could have made a gin and tonic for her sister and added the arsenic before she went out. Of course, there's no proof about that either, that she went out, I mean, but somehow I don't imagine she would sit around watching her sister die. Far better to go to the pictures, as she said, and come back to be horrified by what she found.'

'But surely the glass on the draining board is a sort of proof that there was a visitor.'

'There's no proof of anything, unfortunately. That's something else we've only got Fran's word for too, that Veronica was a compulsively tidy person. And she told us she wouldn't accept the inheritance at any price, but there's nothing to stop her changing her mind about that. I can think of a hundred valid reasons for her to do so . . . that she should respect old Mr Keats's wishes for instance. And in any case if the thing came to trial that wouldn't matter, because it would be just what everyone expected her to say.'

Jenny got up and went back to the kitchen, taking with her the almost empty casserole and returning a moment or two later with a bowl of fruit and some cheese. While she was gone Antony had refilled both glasses. 'Is Roger coming this evening?' he asked as she sat down again.

'Yes, I should think he'd be here any minute.' She paused and smiled at him. 'Is there an ulterior motive behind that question, Antony?'

'Financial matters,' said Antony vaguely. 'They're his thing, aren't they?'

'But you asked him about the Keatses a few days ago.'

'Yes, but it was very casual, just what the general impression of them is. I'm going to ask him to dig just a little bit deeper into their affairs.'

Jenny looked doubtful, but made no protest. They were just finishing their cheese when Roger tapped perfunctorily at the outer door and let himself in.

On Tuesday morning there were documents to peruse, too many and too complicated for Maitland's taste. Sir Nicholas was still in court, and had announced his intention of lunching with his friend Bruce Halloran, so Antony took a chance and telephoned Maurice Keats at his office in the city. To his surprise his suggestion that they lunch together was received without apparent surprise and even with a degree of cordiality. He arranged to meet the other man at Astroff's at twelve-thirty.

Maurice Keats turned out to be a tallish, bulky man, perhaps in his late fifties, his hair grey but still thick, though it was beginning to recede at the temples. It soon became evident that his lack of surprise was quite natural to him, he seemed to have a very calm disposition, the sort of person that nothing could shake. They exchanged platitudes until the waiter had brought their drinks, when Antony said, smiling, 'I can't help feeling it's extraordinarily good of you to take the time to see me.'

'I must admit to some curiosity,' said Maurice. (Maitland had fallen into the habit of thinking of the various members of the family by their Christian names, it seemed to be the only way to distinguish them.) He sipped his drink and smiled in his turn, whether because the taste pleased him or out of friendliness Antony couldn't decide. 'First because it's interesting to me to meet a man I've heard so much about one way and another,' – he must have noticed Antony's frown, but went on smoothly – 'and also because I simply can't imagine what you would want to see me about and with such apparent urgency.'

'Just for the moment we're on neutral ground. Your case for the setting aside of your father's latest will lapsed with Veronica Procter's death.'

'And once it is set in motion again it wouldn't be ethical for you to see me?'

'It might be open to misinterpretation. In the meantime, however –'

'Yes, I can see your point in wanting to see me as soon as possible. Bernard Stanley is of the opinion that there is no doubt now about our success. Your client – I presume you're acting for the sister – is unlikely to contest our claim. I'm sure you've explained the circumstances to her, that our Miss Procter, the one we knew, can't benefit from a crime that she herself committed.'

Maitland let a moment or two pass before he replied, and drank a little of the very good scotch that Astroff's kept for their favourite clients. 'That brings me to the point about which I wanted to see you,' he said at last. 'And in case you think I've an axe to grind in the case of the disputed will I'd better explain to you right away that Miss Frances Procter has disclaimed all interest in the legacy. That means that the matter can be quite easily settled in your favour.'

'She might change her mind.'

'She might, but I don't think she will. What does concern her, however, is the allegation that Veronica Procter poisoned your father. I'm sorry to make you think again about such a sad business –' He broke off and waited hopefully.

Maurice Keats too let the silence lengthen. He was frowning a little when he replied. 'I must say that I don't understand you, Mr Maitland. Surely you must realise that the only motive for Veronica Procter's death is that of her heir . . . whom I believe is this Frances you speak of, and that her reason for wanting to prove her sister's innocence is so that she can herself inherit.'

'Yes, I'm afraid that there are a good many people who will put that construction on what has happened,' Maitland agreed.

'Including, perhaps, the police,' said Maurice.

'Including them. Have you ever met Frances Procter?'

'No. If the sisters met while Veronica was with us it must have been in town.'

'Well, I can assure you that her character is very different from her sister's. To put it bluntly I don't believe for a moment that Veronica Procter died at her hand. And I think her statement that she wants nothing to do with your father's money is quite sincere.'

'You say nothing about my father's possible murderer. You're asking me to believe in Veronica's innocence, but you surely must have realised the corollary to that.'

'I haven't said I believe in Veronica's innocence, only that Fran would like to prove it.'

'And you're acting on her behalf.'

'In a purely unofficial capacity, and I'm not trying to prove anything but the truth. If Veronica did poison your father, as I admit seems the obvious answer, I think it would be better that her sister should understand it clearly rather than always wonder whether it was a false accusation.'

'Your questions have nothing to do with the fact that this girl may be charged with her sister's murder?'

'I won't say that. To prove Veronica innocent might help her in the dispute over the will, as you yourself have pointed out, but it might even be detrimental to her if she was defending herself on a charge of murder.'

'Then I can't quite see your point in agreeing to –'

'To meddle is my uncle's word for it,' said Maitland cheerfully. 'And my only motive is to set her mind at rest . . . one way or the other.' Under certain circumstances that might prove to be true, he could only hope that if it weren't the lie would be forgiven him. 'As I said, I think the most likely thing is that I shan't be able to give her the assurance she wants.'

'No, I don't think you will. You realise, of course, that the alternative to Veronica's guilt would be that of some member of my family?'

'If you mean because of the financial motive, we'd have to add the housekeeper and the cook and her husband, wouldn't we? There are, however, many motives for murder besides financial

103

ones, though I admit,' he added, smiling again, 'that a financial one would be the most likely to occur to a man engaged in your profession.'

Maurice returned his smile and this time it seemed with real amusement. 'I've got an odd feeling you're sincere about this, Mr Maitland,' he said, 'and as I'm quite confident that the truth can't do my family anything but good I'll answer your questions if you like.'

'That's extraordinarily good of you.' Antony didn't trouble to hide his astonishment though he hoped that his embarrassment over this quite unwarranted expression of trust didn't show. 'I must say it's more than I have a right to expect. Shall we get our meal first and then talk over our coffee?'

'That seems a good idea.'

So they ordered their meal and talked of neutral subjects until the plates were removed and their coffee set before them. 'Tell me what you thought about Veronica Procter,' Antony invited then.

'She was a damn fine nurse.'

'Yes, but as a person?'

'A little touchy, but always perfectly polite and helpful.'

'She was with you for three years?'

'Yes, more or less.' He leaned forward, suddenly very earnest. 'During that time, Mr Maitland, she was very often alone with my father. That's why – though in my presence and as far as I know in the presence of all the other members of the family her attitude was always perfectly correct – I thought she must have taken the opportunity to influence him into thinking ill of us. You see I couldn't in honesty say that I'd any doubts about his mental capacity, it had to be that he'd been deceived in some way.'

'There'd never been any question of his entering a home of some kind?'

'No, certainly not. The house was equipped to make everything easy for him, and after so many years he was perfectly well able to get about. I won't say he was resigned to being in a wheel-chair, or to his degree of dependence on others, but

104

whatever his feelings were he kept them to himself. Besides we've a very comfortable household. My wife and I are past the age of wanting to be alone together all the time, we had all the privacy we needed, and it was pleasant to have our son Stephen there, though as you may have heard he's a civil engineer and that takes him abroad a good deal. In fact he just returned from a few months on the continent a week after my father died. It was a great shock to him as well as to the rest of us, but he thought he'd better finish up the job quickly and come home rather than fly back just for the funeral.'

'I'm sure it must have been a great comfort to Mrs Keats and yourself to have him with you, particularly when all this trouble arose about the will.'

'Yes, it was,' Maurice agreed. 'Of course, like every other young man he isn't constantly under foot. I expect we'll be losing him altogether before long, he's engaged to a very fine young woman, Sally Hargreaves. We shall miss him, of course, but we couldn't have wanted a better match for him. Sally is personal assistant to Sir George Challoner who is the chairman of the British Iron Corporation. Sometimes I think she could run the whole firm single-handed.'

'Will she mind his frequent absences?' asked Maitland. He was still doing his best to fall into his companion's mood.

'Oh, I think she'll give up her own work and accompany him. That's what she says anyway. There's no real need for her to continue, even with the very high expectations young people seem to have these days they'll be in no financial difficulty. Any more – in case you're wondering about that, Mr Maitland – than our firm is in difficulties.'

'I wasn't thinking about that at all,' said Antony, this time perfectly truthfully, because having asked Roger to look into the matter he was quite content to await the result. 'Is your nephew, Julian, who I believe works with you, also engaged?'

'He's younger than Stephen, and they haven't – they haven't formalised the relationship yet, though I expect they will one of these days, they seem very much in love. A girl called Jean

Ingelow,' he added in answer to Maitland's inquiring look. 'She works for my sister-in-law, who's a fashion consultant, and like Stephen is out of the country a good deal, though I seem to detect a certain lack of enthusiasm for these trips on her part lately. I think it must be quite six months since she left London.'

'That's Mrs Ralph Keats?'

'Yes, Blythe.' He produced the name without any self-consciousness, so that Antony supposed rather doubtfully that perhaps over the years you could get used to anything.

'Is that her business name?' he asked.

'She uses it for business certainly, but it is also as far as I know her given name,' said Maurice. 'But we seem to have wandered rather far from the subject.'

'Not really, because as head of the family I was going to ask you if you'd have any objection to my seeking these various people out. Each one will see things with a slightly different perspective, and though I'm afraid I shan't have anything very consoling to tell Fran Procter when I finish my inquiries, I think it's better for her to face up to the worst.'

'Yes, I understand. You may not find them all quite so co-operative as you have found me, Mr Maitland.'

'I couldn't hope for that. You've been very kind indeed. But I think if you would explain the situation to them, why I'm asking questions, they would understand–'

'That it might raise suspicions in your mind if they refuse to talk to you,' said Maurice good-humouredly.

'Even if I was thinking that I hope I wouldn't be quite so tactless as to let it show.'

'No, I'm sure you wouldn't.' Maurice stopped for a moment before going on. 'I'll do what I can for you, but I make no promises.'

'I think you'll see what I mean when I ask my two final questions. They both concern things about which other members of your family may well be able to enlighten me more fully than you can. The first is about where your father took his meals.'

106

'Why with the rest of us of course, as did Miss Procter. His digestion had never troubled him, and he ate exactly the same things as the rest of us. Or perhaps I should say we ate the same as he did, because Mrs Grant was very much inclined, in conjunction with our cook Daisy, to give us the things he liked best. But there was no question of any monkey-business at the table.'

'No, I'm sure of it. I understand though that, during the time Miss Procter was with him at least, he did suffer from time to time from bilious attacks.'

'Not that I ever heard of, not until the last months of his life. Very slight at first, and then rather more unpleasant for him. The doctor seemed to think that perfectly natural, talked of a vitamin deficiency and so on. And naturally that was all the more reason for my not being surprised at his getting gastric influenza. Doctor Walton had been attending him regularly, and he had no doubts either at that stage, I don't blame him at all for that. It was only later, when the coincidence of father dying so soon after he had changed his will became apparent, that I began to worry about the subject, and finally approached Bernard Stanley.'

'Yes, I can understand that. I don't like coincidences myself.'

'I imagine you'd like to ask me whether any of us knew about the will before my father's death. The answer is that we didn't.'

'No, I'm sure it was something he'd want to keep to himself. Have you yourself any inkling, Mr Keats, why he should have done such a thing?'

'Because he'd got it into his head that we wanted to put him in an old people's home, in which case I'd ask for a power of attorney over his affairs. Naturally, there was no truth in that at all, but what did surprise me particularly was that Veronica should have profited from his sudden distrust of his own people. If he'd wanted to cut us out he would have been far more likely to have done so in favour of a charity of some sort. I can name any number of good causes that were very near to his heart, to which he gave regularly and generously. That's why it seemed there must have been some influence or other brought to bear.'

'Yes, I'm afraid that's only too reasonable. Now, during his last illness – '

'Veronica was in constant attendance, my wife told me she didn't even take her normal time off on the Thursday. I daresay any of us might have given him a sip of water when visiting him, but my impression is that that would have been in most cases in Veronica's presence, she stayed very close to his side as I've already said. Certainly as far as opportunity goes there's no doubt she was in the most favoured position to produce his symptoms and final death.'

'I'm sorry, Mr Keats, this must be very painful for you. Do you mind adding to your kindness by telling me what you know about Veronica's relationship with her sister?'

'I knew there was a sister, that's absolutely all.'

'So far as we can tell Veronica Procter hadn't made a will. Of course something may turn up in that direction, but it seems doubtful now.'

'In which case the sister will inherit?'

'Anything that she could legitimately leave her. And that brings me to one other point, and this really is the last, Mr Keats. Do you know anything about Veronica's friends?'

'Nothing at all, but that's where our young people might be able to help you. She was friendly with all of them, they'd include her in their outings when she wasn't on duty and any one of them may well know something about her other acquaintances.'

'That would be,' Maitland consulted the notes he had been making, a spider's scrawl as far as Maurice could see looking at them upside down, 'your son Stephen and his fiancée, Miss Sally Hargreaves; and your nephew Julian, with his friend Jean Ingelow?'

'That's right. Actually I think you'll find them all quite co-operative, certainly none of us would want to see an innocent girl blamed for what happened to Veronica. I was afraid at first that you had some doubt in your mind as to whether one of us had been responsible – '

'No apparent motive,' said Maitland shaking his head, which again was true though perhaps misleading.

'– just as I'm afraid we all assumed that Frances Procter was the guilty party.'

'I'm very much obliged to you, Mr Keats.' He signalled the waiter and smiled suddenly across at his companion. 'Let's have another cup of coffee, just to celebrate the fact that we're still on speaking terms,' he said.

'That would be very welcome. Meanwhile, when do you want to see the rest of us?'

'As soon as possible, though I'm afraid this afternoon's out of the question. Tomorrow and Thursday I'm free, if that isn't too short notice.'

'I'll do a little advance publicity on your behalf immediately,' Maurice promised. 'Can I leave a message at your office – at your chambers, I should say – about convenient times and so on. By the way,' he looked all round him rather as if he expected to find some other members of the legal profession lurking nearby, 'I thought barristers never went anywhere without a solicitor in attendance.'

'Like sharks,' said Maitland vaguely. 'That's true enough, but not in a case like this which is, so far, purely a friendly matter.' The waiter came then with their refills, and again the talk turned to other matters.

II

The afternoon passed quickly. There is no denying that Maitland was relieved to have got on to friendly terms with Maurice Keats so comparatively easily. His explanations – his rather difficult explanations – had been made, and now with any luck Keats would pass them on to the other people he wanted to see. It was a fairly safe bet that not all of them would receive him quite so

109

amiably, but that didn't worry him overmuch. It was not too difficult to plunge himself into the work that was waiting for him, and by the time he piled the documents tidily together and replaced the last reference book on the shelf he felt he could congratulate himself on having got most of the meat out of the facts at his disposal both from the Forgery Act of 1913 and the Counterfeit Currency (Convention) Act of 1935.Whether his client would be equally pleased with the result of his researches was, of course, another matter. He had been clever undoubtedly, but perhaps a little too clever.

Sir Nicholas was almost certain to have gone straight home from court, and when Antony also arrived at the house in Kempenfeldt Square he found he'd been right about that. Gibbs, as was quite normal, rebuked his tardiness with the words, 'Sir Nicholas and Lady Harding joined Mrs Maitland half an hour ago.' Just as he would have greeted any earlier arrival, again by implication, by conveying that this somehow constituted a dereliction of duty. Maitland, whose walk home had not diminished his sense of self-satisfaction, replied cheerfully, and made his way quickly up the stairs.

Sir Nicholas also he found in a mellow mood, having routed his friend Bruce Halloran very effectively that day in court. He'd obviously been awaiting his nephew's arrival to give a blow-by-blow account of the action, so for once there were no immediate questions for Antony to answer as to his own doings, and as shop was strictly forbidden at the dinner table it wasn't until they were all settled down around the fire again, that the matter came up.

'You haven't said anything about this insane idea of yours, Antony, of trying to prove Veronica Procter innocent of murdering her employer. Does that mean you've thought better of it?'

'As a matter of fact, Uncle Nick, I had lunch with Maurice Keats today.'

'Should have thought you'd have found conversation a little difficult,' said Vera in her gruff way.

110

Antony smiled at her. 'Not nearly as difficult as I'd expected,' he confided. 'In fact –'

'Can't have told him the whole truth,' said Vera, shaking her head.

'Well . . . no. I didn't emphasise the fact that if Veronica wasn't guilty most likely one of his near relations was,' Maitland agreed, 'though it was obvious enough that he took the point and didn't greatly resent it. I had to give him the impression, of course, that my questions were more concerned with helping Fran Procter if the police decided to arrest her, because the family with whom Veronica had been living for three years might be more likely to know something of her affairs, probably a good deal more than her sister did.'

'Take off my hat to you,' said Vera, who never wore one. 'Didn't think you could get away with it.'

'I don't think you could say I got away with anything,' said Maitland slowly. 'Except that he's promised to explain what I want to the other members of the family, so that they'll have no hesitation about talking to me. But what I can't decide is whether he was talkative out of sheer friendliness, or because he was trying to hide something. That's a distinct possibility. He confirmed the doctor's opinion that there was nothing at all wrong with his father's digestion until the last three months of his life, when he suffered some very minor attacks, and then some slightly more serious ones immediately preceding his last illness. That makes Veronica a liar.'

'It increases the likelihood of her guilt,' said Sir Nicholas judicially. 'If the first attacks coincided with the start of her campaign to get herself made his heir, she wouldn't have wanted to run the risk of really hurting him until the new will had been made, and as a nurse she'd know well enough how to achieve her effects. You do see that, don't you, my dear boy?'

'Yes, I see that, Uncle Nick, and I agree with you. I'll tell you exactly what was said as far as I remember it, but as you'll see it gets me absolutely nowhere.'

'If your purpose is to establish Frances Procter's innocence, rather than her sister's, I must say I agree with you,' said his uncle when he had finished speaking. 'Do you really think she's in danger of arrest?'

'I don't know. It's difficult to see what good Veronica's death would do the Keats family, they didn't even have to know that Fran would refuse the legacy, it was obvious that in view of the facts that had come to light they'd have no difficulty at all in setting aside the new will. As for some outsider coming into the affair at this stage . . . I just don't believe it, though I'm glad Maurice seems to think I do. But that's enough of that for tonight. I may have to immerse myself in the whole wretched business again tomorrow, but just now I'm sure we've better things to talk about.'

But he had spoken too soon. Roger's arrival a quarter of an hour later coincided with the ringing of the telephone. Antony went to answer it, listened for a moment and then said, 'I'll come round immediately,' and slammed down the receiver again. 'That was Johnny Lund,' he said, turning to face the room again. 'I didn't get any details, but he says someone's tried to murder Fran. Would you mind driving me, Roger? It would be far quicker than looking for a taxi.'

It was not in Roger's nature to refuse any call to action. They were both downstairs and into the Jensen with only the sketchiest of farewells. 'Chelsea,' said Antony, and gave his friend precise directions. But once they were on their way he relaxed and looked at his watch. 'Nine-fifteen,' he said. 'You're late tonight.'

Roger's attention was on his driving. 'I bumped into Jeremy,' he said absently, 'and he kept me talking. Do you suppose Johnny had the presence of mind to send for the doctor? I gather from the way you rushed me out of the place that he'd got in a bit of a panic.'

'That's what I was afraid of, but he did say he'd taken care of that. And there's no use asking me exactly what happened to Fran, because I didn't wait to hear.'

After that they drove in silence until Roger, who had a knack of finding parking spots where no-one else could, drew up almost outside the house. 'I'll wait for you,' he offered.

'No, come with me if you don't mind. I don't know quite what we're going to find,' Antony said, 'and another witness may be useful.'

What they did find was a scene of confusion. The upstairs flat, or maisonnette as an estate agent would have called it, had its own front door leading immediately to a steep flight of stairs. Johnny Lund came down to let them in with a distinctly straws-in-the-hair look about him, as Antony said later to Jenny. 'Thank God you're here,' he said. 'This is perfectly awful. There was Fran on the floor and I thought at first she was dead.'

'You're babbling, Johnny,' Maitland told him. 'Pull yourself together and tell me quickly, did the doctor get here?'

'Yes, he's with her now.'

'Well, we can't stand here talking on the doorstep. Let us in, there's a good chap.'

Johnny turned obligingly and began to walk up the stairs talking all the time. 'I didn't know what to do,' he said. 'The doctor said I must call the police, because it was obvious there'd been an attempted burglary. So I called the local chaps, they haven't got here yet, but I thought perhaps as you know Sykes so well, Antony, it might be as well to tell him. Because obviously it proves Fran couldn't have had anything to do with what's been happening.'

'We'll think about Sykes in a moment,' said Antony. They'd reached the head of the stairs now and Johnny led the way into the small sitting-room. 'Until I know what happened –' He broke off, looking around him.

'They're in the bedroom,' said Johnny as though divining his thoughts.

'Then you can take a deep breath and tell me just what happened. You say somebody tried to kill Fran Procter. Is she all right?'

'The doctor says she will be, probably a slight concussion, he said. I'd carried her into the bedroom by the time he got here, of course, but when he'd had a look at her he came out again and

113

asked me where I'd found her. It was just inside the room here, just inside the door. He said perhaps she tripped coming in and hit her head on the table over there, but by that time I'd had a look around, and you can see for yourself somebody had been searching the bureau over there. Besides there was that bit of rock, or whatever it is, that she used to prop the door open. It wasn't in its usual place and when I found her the door had swung to until it was touching her shoulder. So that was when the doctor decided that she'd interrupted a burglar, and he'd hit her over the head with it and got away.'

'Any chance of fingerprints?'

'Just look at it.' But Antony was already doing so, and had realised that the question was a foolish one. Whatever the thing was made of – a relic of some seaside holiday perhaps? – the surface was nowhere near smooth enough to have taken any identifiable prints.

'I see,' he said, not very happily. But before he could go any further there was a thunderous knocking on the door below.

'That'll be the police,' said Johnny unnecessarily. 'I'd better go and let them in, hadn't I?'

'It might be advisable.' As soon as Johnny had disappeared he turned to Farrell. 'Will you hold the fort here for a moment, Roger?' he asked. 'I'm not absolutely sure which is the bedroom, probably this door over here.' He had crossed to it as he spoke, and tapped lightly on the panel. A moment later it was flung open.

'Who the devil are you?' inquired the man who had opened it, a rather short tubby man who was presumably the doctor.

'A friend of Miss Procter's,' Antony told him.

'Thought you didn't look like the police.'

'How is she? May I come in?'

'If you like. And what the world's coming to,' he added, turning towards the bed, 'what with young girls knowing no better than to live alone, and thieves breaking in at this time of the evening –'

'Yes, it's all very dreadful,' said Maitland meaninglessly. 'Can

114

you tell me, doctor, what time you think the–the incident occurred? How long had Miss Procter been unconscious when you saw her?'

'Can only make a guess at it, of course,' said the doctor, who was reminding Antony minute by minute more of Vera both in his gruff way of speaking and the way he cut his sentences short. 'Haven't had a chance to talk to the girl yet, but I'd guess the attack took place somewhere about eight o'clock.'

'And what's the damage?'

'Nasty lump on the side of her head, painful I should think.' He turned to Fran, whose eyes were open now, and added more gently, 'How are you feeling now, my dear?'

'Horrible,' said Fran weakly. Her eyes went past the doctor to meet Maitland's concerned gaze. 'I don't understand,' she said.

'What don't you understand, Fran?'

'The bureau . . . there's nothing there. I don't have anything at all that's valuable.'

'Never mind about it now. Just lie still, I'm sure that's what the doctor would want. But before the police get here–'

'Again?' said Fran.

'They haven't got here yet,' said the doctor, 'or only just,' he amended, hearing some signs of movement in the living-room. 'Confused that's all,' he added to Antony in a sort of aside.

'May I ask her two questions?'

'Can't do any harm that I can see. You may not get sensible answers though.'

'I'll try. The first thing is, Fran, what time did you come in?'

'Soon after eight, I think.'

'Was everything as usual?'

'Until I opened the sitting-room door. Then I saw the bureau. I'm not dreaming, am I?' she appealed to the doctor.

'Certainly not about that, my dear,' he replied, picking up her hand and patting it.

115

'The flap was torn off, and all the papers thrown about. But I don't own anything that anybody could possibly want,' she said again.

'And after that?'

'I was just standing staring,' she said very slowly, 'and then I don't remember any more.'

'We think somebody hit you. Did you see him?'

'No, there was nobody.'

'Post traumatic amnesia,' said the doctor briskly. 'She might remember at any moment, or she might never remember what happened.'

'I see,' said Maitland again. 'Can you leave your patient for a moment, doctor? I think the police are here from the sound of it, and I'm sure they'd like a word with you.'

'In just a moment.' The doctor was rummaging in his bag. 'Is there anyone who could stay with you tonight?' he asked.

'No, I can't think of anybody. I'll be quite all right now.'

'Then we must rely on your friend here to make sure everything's locked up safely after everyone leaves. Meanwhile, my dear, you take these two tablets, they'll make you sleepy and there's no harm in that. Have a good sleep and don't worry about anything. I'll be round again in the morning, and if you have a spare key you can let me have, I'll let myself in.'

'There was Veronica's, but it was in her handbag and the police took it,' said Fran, obviously confirming the doctor's worst suspicions about her mental state. 'But if you can find my handbag you can take mine, I shan't be needing it,' she added, to Antony's relief with a very faint smile.

'I'll look round for it,' the doctor promised. 'I'll just see she has some water,' he added to Antony, 'then I'll be out to see the police.'

'I'll try to see you tomorrow, Fran, when you're feeling better,' said Antony. 'With the doctor's permission, of course.' He took himself off into the sitting-room again, which with the addition of a plain clothes detective and two largish constables seemed very much over-full. Johnny, he was glad to see, had

116

pulled himself together again, and was answering their questions in a grave professional way.

'I didn't notice the exact time I got here,' he was saying, and something in his tone made Antony believe that it was not the first repetition. 'I think it would be about ten or five to nine. I rang the bell downstairs and there was no answer so I tried knocking, and as I knocked the door was swung open a little. I'd no idea if Fran was at home, but whether she was or not that couldn't be right, so I thought I'd better have a look upstairs to see if everything was in order. And that's when I found her, just as I told you.'

The plain clothes man, who was tallish but still succeeded in looking rather like a fox terrier, turned to Antony. 'Are you another friend of Miss Procter's?' he asked rather belligerently.

'Certainly I am.'

'When did you arrive?'

'Not long before you did. With Mr Farrell here.'

'I called them,' said Johnny. 'I called the doctor, because at first I thought she was dead or terribly badly injured, and then I called Mr Maitland. And then the doctor said I should call you.'

'And what do you know about this?' The detective gesticulated towards the broken bureau as he spoke. The flap that was meant to let down for writing had indeed been wrenched off with some force, papers from the pigeon holes were scattered on the floor, and the wood was gouged, so that it looked as if some attempt had been made to remove the pigeon holes forcibly too.

'Nothing at all,' said Johnny. 'How should I?'

'Miss Procter says that she came home soon after eight o'clock,' Antony put in.

'Then I'd better see her.'

'I don't think –' But the doctor emerged from the bedroom at that point to speak for himself.

'No question of talking to the girl tonight,' he said. 'She'll be all right tomorrow but just now she's a little confused.' He conferred for a few moments with the policeman, during which period Antony didn't learn any more than he knew already,

117

dictated his name and address to one of the constables, found Fran's handbag and removed the latch key. 'I'll try this as I go down to make sure it's the right one,' he said to Antony. 'Don't forget now, you're responsible for locking up.'

'I won't forget,' said Maitland mildly. 'But meanwhile,' he added, as the doctor's footsteps receded down the stairs, 'I really think Mr Lund's right and I should give Detective Chief Inspector Sykes a call.'

'Sykes?' said the fox terrier man unbelievingly. 'You don't call in Scotland Yard over a thing like this, we don't even know if anything's been taken.'

'I can see I shall have to explain,' said Antony resignedly. He did so as briefly as possible. The plain clothes man was looking thoughtful when he had finished, but made no further objection to his using the telephone.

III

'But I wasn't as pleased with the idea of calling Sykes as Johnny was,' said Antony much later, 'though I could see it had to be done.' He had got back to Kempenfeldt Square to find Sir Nicholas and Vera still keeping Jenny company. 'You see all he can think of is that this proves Fran had nothing to do with any of the previous incidents, whereas I'm afraid the police will take it in exactly the opposite way.'

'Is she really all right alone?' asked Jenny anxiously. 'I suppose Roger went straight to the theatre –'

'Yes, he left us some time ago.'

'– but I could get a taxi and go round and stay with her.'

'No need, love. Johnny's bedded down on the sofa. And I shouldn't like,' he added thoughtfully, 'to be any stray marauder who tried to get at Fran tonight.'

'That's good,' said Jenny. 'Now you can tell us why you didn't want to call Inspector Sykes. I expect he came?'

118

'Eventually, and as Johnny had offered to stay the night there was no need for me to stick around any longer. I left them busy going over the flat for fingerprints, though I shouldn't think they had a hope in hell of finding any. Everyone knows enough to wear gloves nowadays. I expect they'll want to do the bedroom tomorrow, though there was no sign in there – I could tell them that – that anybody had been searching. That seems to have been confined to the bureau and it puzzles me rather.'

'Going to tell us,' said Vera, immediately sending Antony's mind scurrying back to the earlier part of the evening and his conversation with the doctor, 'why Johnny's idea of sending for Sykes didn't appeal to you as much as it did to him.'

'Look at it from their point of view,' said Antony. 'You'll agree with me about this, Uncle Nick. She was hurt, but not seriously so, apparently by a blow from the door-stop that was lying nearby, though as her skin wasn't broken there's no positive proof of that. But I think if the doctor were asked on oath whether the injury might not have been self-inflicted if she were desperate enough he wouldn't be able to say for certain either way. The fox terrier man – the dectective who first got there I mean – obviously suspected Johnny of something or other. What's to stop the rest of them?'

'Sykes isn't one to jump to conclusions,' said Sir Nicholas.

'No, but he has Briggs to reckon with.'

'In that case, if they suspect Johnny of having a hand in the affair it would obviously be with your connivance,' said Sir Nicholas. For once in his life he forebore to take his recriminations any further but heaved himself out of his chair, and held out a hand to pull Vera to her feet. 'Give your husband a drink, my dear,' he said to Jenny. 'There's nothing we can do tonight, we must just wait to see what tomorrow will bring.'

Wednesday, May 1st

I

The following morning Maitland was on the phone to Fran Procter's flat as early as he felt was reasonable. Johnny answered promptly, sounding much more like himself. Quite in command, in fact, of both the situation and his own feelings.

'Yes, she's awake,' he said in answer to Antony's query, 'and the doctor's been. He seemed quite impressed with her progress – what did she say last night to make him think she was rambling? He just told her to take a couple of aspirin tablets if the headache persisted. I've made her some tea and persuaded her to take the aspirins with it, though she didn't really want to and in fact she does seem quite lively again. The doctor said it was quite all right to leave her, so I'm going to the office in a minute or two. The old beggar gave me rather an odd look when I said I was Fran's solicitor.'

'I don't wonder,' said Antony. 'It isn't part of the normal solicitor-client relationship – '

'Well,' said Johnny rather defensively, 'I couldn't leave her. She's promised to be careful about locking up after me when I go.'

'Last night after I left – ' Maitland didn't bother to finish the sentence, but his tone held a question.

'Two things,' said Johnny. 'The first one isn't anything to be surprised at really, whoever did his best to tear the bureau to pieces wore gloves obviously. The other is more of a puzzle, how did he get in? Fran told me this morning there are only two keys . . . hers, which she lent to the doctor last night, and Veronica's which was still in her handbag when the police took it away. She's also willing to swear on a stack of Bibles that she locked the door when she went out, though as far as I can see the only explanation is that she didn't.'

'You're telling me there were no signs of forcible entry.'

'No signs at all. And there's a dead bolt on the door downstairs.'

'Yes, that is a puzzle,' Antony agreed. 'Anything else?'

'Fran made a tour of the place after the doctor had been, and while I was making the tea,' said Johnny. 'She says there's nothing whatever missing, though of course she couldn't be sure about every scrap of paper that had been in the bureau. That belonged to Veronica by the way, but of course she'd nowhere to keep it, always living in other people's houses, so Fran stored it for her. There was nothing of Veronica's there though, and Fran had only used it for bills and receipts and unanswered letters . . . nothing important.'

'Curiouser and curiouser,' said Antony. 'Well, I'd better let you get on with your day's work, Johnny. What about Sykes and Mayhew?'

'Obviously they'll want to hear what Fran has to say at first hand, but they promised to let me know what time they're going to visit her, so that I can be there. But it must be obvious now—mustn't it?—that the same person who killed Veronica was searching the flat last night and Fran interrupted him.'

'It may be obvious to us, Johnny,' said Maitland reluctantly, 'but I think I ought to warn you that I'm not at all sure it'll be quite so clear to the police. I'm not sure until I get to chambers how my day is going to be arranged, Maurice Keats promised to leave a message for me about which of the family I'd find at home and at what times. But if it can be arranged I'd like to be present when they talk to Fran. Perhaps you

121

could persuade Sykes that late this afternoon would give her a better chance of recovering herself.'

'Well, I suppose . . . there's no need to tell him that the doctor more or less gave her a clean bill of health,' said Johnny. He sounded worried now.

'I don't think I'd say too much about the doctor's opinion either way,' Antony advised. 'I've got a suspicion they'll be talking to him themselves.'

Johnny, of course, demanded an instant explanation and Antony gave him his own ideas as to what the police interpretation of the new development might be, very much as he had done on getting home last night, though rather more gently. Johnny was obviously anxious, but showed no signs of going to pieces again. Antony rang off feeling rather like a murderer himself, but there had been nothing for it, the other man had to know what they might be up against.

When he got to chambers the message from Maurice Keats was that his wife Isabel would be at home all the morning and willing to see Mr Maitland. Also, Stephen had agreed to stay at home until after Antony's visit. That prompted an immediate call to Roger Farrell at his office in the city. 'I need a chauffeur and confidant,' said Antony abruptly. 'Any chance of your being free this morning?'

'All day if you like,' said Roger, and wasted no time in asking questions. 'I'll pick you up at the top of Middle Temple Lane in half an hour,' he promised.

As always he was prompt to the minute. 'Where to?' he asked as Antony slid into the passenger's seat beside him.

'Wimbledon.' He consulted the inevitable envelope with the address scribbled on it and read it out. 'I think that's near the Common,' he added doubtfully.

'Don't worry, I can find it,' said Roger. 'I've a client who lives a few doors away, and I've been there to see him. Is that where Maurice Keats lives?'

122

'Yes, it is.'

'Well, if the address is any guideline there's nothing wrong with him financially. All the houses down there are enormous, with extensive grounds, and the upkeep alone must be quite a consideration.'

'The house belonged to his father,' Antony pointed out, 'and as far as I can tell he made his pile and stuck to it like glue. Even with half the residuary estate Maurice would be in clover, but without it, if the firm's not doing too well perhaps, it might mean a change of lifestyle. That could apply to the other members of the family, of course, and even the hundred thousand each that the two grandsons were to get isn't to be sneezed at.'

'I can quite see that any one of them might have killed him in expectation of plenty,' said Roger, 'and only found out too late about the new will. But you can't deny that Veronica Procter had the best opportunity.'

'I don't deny it.'

'Well then, Antony, I don't think you can have it both ways. If Veronica killed the old man there was absolutely no reason for one of the family to kill her. They must have known the mere suggestion of foul play would be enough to get the will overset.'

'Only the motive you pointed out yourself . . . revenge.'

'You didn't believe me then and I don't for a moment think you believe me now,' said Roger. 'For that matter, I don't think much of the idea myself.'

'Nothing makes sense at this stage,' Antony agreed. 'We've got to make some attempt to produce an explanation though and that pretty quickly.' He had had no opportunity to explain to Roger the night before his opinion of what the police attitude might be, and he did so now, in as few words as possible.

'Why the hurry?' Farrell asked him. 'If she is arrested the trial couldn't come on immediately.'

'No, that's not quite the point, though I'd hate to think of her in prison waiting for her appearance in court. She's a nice girl, Roger, quite unlike her sister. But the thing is, you see, if Sykes is right in his estimate of Superintendent Brigg's feelings about this case it might be that both Johnny and I would have to stand down as her representatives. If someone else took over there's no saying that they'd see things our way, and even if they did, even if they whole-heartedly came to believe in Fran's innocence, they'd almost certainly resent my interference.'

'Yes, I can quite see that. All the same, Antony, you're far more likely than anyone I know to be able to clear the matter up,' said Roger, who had his own reasons for having a good deal of faith in his friend's ability to see as far through a brick wall as the next man. 'If you could produce some evidence, the fact that Briggs hates your guts wouldn't have the slightest effect on the court.'

'That's what I'm always telling Uncle Nick,' Antony agreed. 'The trouble is in that "if" There's no evidence except Fran's that anybody visited Veronica the night she died, and she herself wasn't badly hurt last night.'

'Badly enough to render her unconscious for a considerable time.'

'Yes, but there's only her word for that too. It could easily be maintained that the whole thing was a clumsy attempt to prove her innocence, with or without the help of an accomplice.'

'Good lord, Antony, you don't think Johnny – ?'

'No, I don't, but even about Johnny I'm not absolutely certain. He's certainly showing a very protective attitude towards her now.'

'It sounds to me like a pretty good mess,' said Roger. 'And as you didn't ask Johnny to drive you I take it you want a witness to these talks who might be considered unbiased. But how are you going to explain me away to Isabel Keats?

Remember I have been introduced to her and she may well remember my face.'

'That's easy. I shall say I thought she'd feel more comfortable talking to me in the presence of someone she already knew,' said Antony blandly. 'I don't know whether she'll believe me, of course.'

And that's exactly what he did when they got to the house, (which was just as large and opulent-looking as Roger had led him to expect) and were shown into Isabel Keats's presence. She showed no sign of surprise, nor did she ask for any explanation of their errand. Her husband, Antony reflected, must have been extraordinarily persuasive.

From Veronica's description Antony had expected Isabel Keats to be something of a fashion plate, the sort of woman who felt it would be beneath her to soil her hands with any kind of household work, but the impression he gained was rather different. A handsome, well-dressed woman certainly, but one who took no part in household affairs and whom nobody expected to help look after an ailing father-in-law, not because she was unkind or felt it would be beneath her, but simply because it had never occurred to her to do so.

'Maurice says you feel it would be better for Veronica's sister to know the truth about her,' she said, almost before they were all seated, and if this was rather a free translation of his talk with her husband, Maitland wasn't going to dispute it, even if she'd given him the opportunity of doing so. 'Of course,' she prattled on, 'I'm only too glad to help you. I think it's very important to face up to things, don't you? It's not that I was ever in any doubt of what happened, but I can quite understand the sister feeling differently. Naturally it never occurred to me . . . well, you don't expect people you know to be murderers do you? But there's no doubt Veronica was a very odd girl.'

'Perhaps you could explain that to us, Mrs Keats,' Antony suggested. 'I'd be very interested in your opinion of her.'

('Flattery, shameless flattery,' said Roger later, and when Antony protested added by way of explanation, 'Not what you said exactly, but the way you said it.')

'There's no doubt she looked after father wonderfully,' Isabel told them. 'Naturally that was the first consideration, but when I realise now that she was probably making up to him all the time I wonder how we could all have been so blind. Of course she took her meals with us – she was quite the lady – except during the last few days when father was ill, and she was with us for three years, and perfectly friendly always in a rather distant sort of way, but not a girl to talk about her own affairs. Not at all open.'

'So you can't tell me anything about her family or friends?'

'I knew she had a sister. I never thought they were very close, though Veronica was a very practical girl and I think, to tell you the truth, that she rather resented the fact that her sister wanted to be an artist. Painting pictures, that's how she put it, nothing more than a hobby really, nothing she should want to devote her life to. And in the meantime she seemed to be perfectly comfortably off, and had her own home and everything, while Veronica . . . no-one can deny that nursing is very hard work.'

'Was there a great deal to be done for your father-in-law?'

'Tiresome things,' said Isabel, and for once didn't amplify the statement.

'Yes, I'm sure,' said Maitland. 'How was his general health, apart from his – his disability?'

'Oh, excellent. We were all sure he'd live to be a hundred. Then during the last few months there were a few little upsets, nothing that worried any of us unduly. But now it seems quite obvious that it was that girl, preparing our minds as it were for that she was going to do.'

'But nothing before, say, three months before his death?'

'Nothing at all.'

'You were telling us, Mrs Keats, about Veronica Procter's

friends.'

She made a kind of despairing gesture, 'I don't know anything about them,' she said. 'I told you she wasn't a girl to confide in one. Only sometimes the younger members of the family – if Stephen was home for instance and Sally had come to dine with us, or if Julian brought his girl-friend, Jean, to dinner – they'd ask Veronica to go out and see a film with them afterwards or something like that. I think it was Sally Hargreaves's idea really, she's engaged to Stephen you know, a perfectly dear girl. And she did say to me once or twice that she thought that Veronica was a very lonely person. And of course it was perfectly all right with me, father never liked to go to bed early, Veronica could settle him quite well when she came home. And in the meantime if he needed anything Mrs Grant was very capable.'

'These occasions, I gather, were when she was supposed to be on duty, not on her days off?'

'That's right. She never mentioned what she did then, never a word. Even if I asked her how she'd enjoyed her day she'd just say she'd had a very pleasant time or something like that. No details.'

'Did you find that old Mr Keats became a little testy during those last months?'

'A little perhaps with other people, but never with me.'

'There was never any question of his going to live somewhere where medical attention might be more freely available?'

'You're thinking of that nonsense Veronica put into his mind. There was never any question of that, how could there have been? He was perfectly sane even if she made him believe things that weren't true, and the idea that Maurice should be given power of attorney and take everything into his own hands was just absurd. Besides, we were all very fond of him, and he was no trouble, no trouble at all.'

'Then may we turn to a subject that you may find distressing? Your father-in-law's last illness – '

'It was distressing when he died, but we didn't think at first that would happen, you know. Gastric 'flu, it's not such an uncommon thing, and we always thought he was very strong even though he was nearly eighty.'

'His illness lasted five days I believe.'

'Yes, I think that's about right.'

'His meals during that time – '

'He wasn't eating, I don't think he could keep anything down. But Veronica would ring down to the kitchen sometimes for some warm milk, or some hot sweet tea to try to keep his strength up. I remember very well because there was a little trouble over that, our cook Daisy said it was none of her business to wait on the girl, who had two legs like anybody else and could quite well come and fetch what she wanted. Veronica said, of course, that she couldn't leave her patient, so usually it ended with Mrs Grant taking the tray upstairs, which wasn't her business either.'

'Can you remember any occasion during that period when your father-in-law was left alone?'

'Not to my knowledge. There's a bathroom off his bedroom, and Veronica insisted on sleeping on the sofa under the window. Of course when she was bathing and changing in the morning, she'd be in the bathroom then, but if you're thinking one of the servants might have sneaked in and put something in his carafe of drinking water for instance, Daisy and her husband and Mrs Grant have been with us for years. They're all absolutely reliable.'

Antony didn't bother to point out that neither Daisy nor Mrs Grant would have had any reason for doing such a thing, both of them having been from time to time in control of the hot drinks that were sent up to the sick room. He was anxious not to antagonise Mrs Keats, and only said vaguely, 'No, I was just trying to get a clear picture. You know, Mrs Keats, I can't help being disappointed that Veronica Procter didn't confide in you more about her friends.'

'Yes, Maurice said you were worried that the sister – what's her name –'

'Frances,' Antony murmured.

' – wouldn't realise that the new will wasn't worth the paper it was written on once it was known what Veronica had done. But if you really think it might have been some other of Veronica's friends who killed her, perhaps Stephen or one of the others might be able to help you. Young people can be very difficult nowadays, and she may have talked more freely to someone of her own generation.'

'Yes, that's very possible. I understand from Mr Keats's message that it might be possible to see your son here this morning.'

'Yes, he's in. He just said he'd keep out of the way while we were talking together. It's been a great pleasure to meet you, Mr Maitland, and it was very kind of you, Mr Farrell,' she added to the silent Roger, 'to come along too. But you see it wasn't in the least bit necessary, Mr Maitland isn't at all a frightening person.'

'That's because you've been so helpful,' said Roger, smiling at her. 'You ought to see him with a witness who's trying to hide something.'

'Oh my goodness!' She was quite at ease with them now and thoroughly enjoying the attention. 'I'll just send a message to Stephen to tell him to come in now.' She got up from her chair, and to Antony's great admiration tugged at the old-fashioned bell-pull beside the fireplace. There were plenty of them still around of course, but so few people dared to make use of them.

Mrs Grant appeared in her own unruffled way after quite a short interval. 'I think Mr Stephen is in the study,' Mrs Keats told her. 'Would you mind asking him to come in here?'

Roger swore afterwards that Mrs Grant winked at him as she left the room. That seemed to Antony unlikely, but the housekeeper certainly succeeded in conveying the impression

129

that her mistress's ways amused her. Times might have changed, but none of that change had registered with Isabel Keats, and probably with most of her underlings her calm air of confidence was sufficient to get her wishes respected.

When Stephen Keats came into the room Maitland had again to remind himself that it was a very bad habit to form a mental picture of someone before the actual meeting had taken place. For some reason he had expected casual clothes – perhaps even jeans – and a beard; the young man who came in was darkish and slim and not particularly tall, and would have looked by no means out of place interviewing the most influential of the clients of his father's firm in the city. Was this neatness of his own choice, or was it out of deference to his mother? In any event he had that much in common with Isabel that he greeted them in a friendly way, accepted the explanation of Roger's presence – this time given by his mother, 'So thoughtful of them, my dear' – with equanimity, seated himself and eyed Antony expectantly.

'I'm quite willing to be helpful,' he said, 'but I don't quite see how I can be. Certainly not about Grandfather's death, all I know about that is hearsay. Which I understand is anathema to lawyers,' he added with a smile.

'You were away at the time he died, Mr Keats?'

'Yes, and as I was due home so soon I thought it better not to attend the funeral. That can't do any good anyway, can it? But I don't think there can be any reasonable doubt now about what happened.'

'In any event your presence when you got back must have been very helpful to your parents,' said Antony. If he wished that Isabel would take herself off for a moment, it was obviously impossible to suggest such a thing. 'I'm sure your father explained to you that I feel it better for Miss Frances Procter to know the truth about what her sister did, and that at the same time I'm rather anxious about her own position with regard to Veronica's death. On the face of it one would

130

expect some connection between that and what happened to your grandfather, but I know nothing of Veronica's friends and associates, and that's where I hoped you could help me.'

'I never met Fran,' said Stephen. 'To tell you the truth I don't think Veronica cared for her much even though they were twins. Veronica was a very practical person, you know, and a hell of a good nurse, and I think her sister's occupation was not quite to her taste.'

'Still, she went to stay with her when she left here.'

'I don't suppose she had anywhere else to go. I gather all hell broke loose here as soon as it was known about the new will, but I don't think even Veronica would have had the effrontery to suggest that we should leave while the matter was decided. Besides, Chelsea is convenient, and with Fran upstairs in that studio of hers all day I expect it felt to Veronica as though the place was her own.'

'It's funny that they should look so much alike and yet were so different in temperament.'

'That was something else Veronica didn't altogether like, she said it was no fun at all having an identical twin. I say, there's an idea for you! Have you ever considered that it might not have been Veronica who was poisoned at all?'

'It hadn't occurred to me,' said Maitland, a little taken aback.

'No, but it could have been, couldn't it?' Stephen was warming to the idea. 'Once it was known grandfather had been poisoned Veronica was the obvious suspect. So she poisoned Fran hoping that everyone would think she had committed suicide, either out of remorse or fear, in which case she'd have no more to worry about.'

'I believe an attempt was made to make the death look like suicide,' Antony agreed, 'but it wasn't a very successful one.'

Stephen frowned over that. 'I know the newspapers said the police were treating it as a case of murder, but I don't really understand why.'

'There were several reasons, but the most cogent one, I think, was the bottle that contained the solution of arsenic.'

'What was wrong with it?'

'There were no fingerprints, and whichever of the twins really died,' he added with a faintly amused look, 'I can't see any reason for her to have wiped the bottle clean if she had taken the poison deliberately.'

'That was an oversight, wasn't it?'

'It all depends, I suppose, on how you look at it. That's an interesting idea Mr Keats and I'll certainly bear it in mind, but in the meantime do you think we could assume for the purpose of our discussion that it was Veronica Procter who died. If you're acquainted with any of her friends, or ever heard her talk about them, it would be very helpful to know.'

'That was the funny thing about Veronica, she was as close as a clam about her own affairs. Sally – that's Sally Hargreaves, my fiancée – thought she didn't say much about her private life because she didn't really have one, and that's reasonable enough when you think about it, living always in other people's homes and so on. Can't Fran tell you anything about that, there must have been some people they knew as children?'

'They were brought up in the country somewhere, according to Fran –'

'Or Veronica.'

'According to whichever is still alive,' said Antony obligingly. 'When it was time for Veronica to start her nurse's training their mother was very keen that Fran should come up to London as well, and as she wanted to attend art school, that's just what she did. Since then their parents have died, and they've lost touch with everyone from their old village. There don't seem to be any aunts or uncles or cousins.'

'That fits in pretty well with Sally's ideas, and I think she was sorry for Veronica for all that Veronica was so very self-possessed. She used to suggest we take her out sometimes, we'd go to a film or to the pub round the corner . . . it's perfectly respectable, mother. Dad could take you there and no-one would raise an eyebrow.'

'Thank you, Stephen, I've never seen the point of leaving a perfectly comfortable home –'

'It makes a nice change,' said Stephen, not waiting for her to finish. 'It was a bit of a bore actually having Veronica along, but Sally's too kind-hearted if that's possible, and I think she talked to Jean too. Did Mother mention Jean? It's Jean Ingelow, she works for my Aunt Blythe, and one of these days I expect she'll marry Julian. Anyway sometimes they'd come along as well, and sometimes they'd take Veronica out on their own. I daresay Julian found it as much of a bore as I did, but anything for a quiet life.'

'Mrs Keats told me that these occasions were not on Miss Procter's days off.'

'No, I've no idea what she did with her time then. I told you she was close-mouthed, I wish I could help you but I can't see how.'

'You've been very kind to give us so much of your time,' said Maitland getting up. 'And a few things to think about into the bargain,' he added smiling. 'Do you think Miss Hargreaves . . . you said it was her idea to take Veronica Procter with you sometimes. Do you think there's any chance at all that Veronica might have talked more to her?'

'I suppose there's a chance,' said Stephen. 'Do you mean you'd like to see her?'

'Very much, if you've no objection.'

'Sally has a mind of her own, it wouldn't be up to me to object,' Stephen told him. 'However . . . are you going back to town now?'

'Yes, we are.'

'And is that your car outside the front door?'

'Mine,' said Roger. That knack of his for effacing himself made his return into the conversation almost a shock.

133

'I like the look of it, but it's a make I don't know.'

'A Jensen. I've been driving them for years, but I think this'll be the last. The spares are getting hard to get.'

'Well then, why don't you give me a lift back to town? I'm lunching with Sally and I'm sure she won't mind if you both join us. Then you can ask her your questions, Mr Maitland, and I can tell her my idea about Veronica and Fran. The more I think about it the more I think it's the mostly likely thing to have happened. After all they say the second murder's always much easier than the first.'

'Stephen!' said Isabel rather faintly. Then she smiled at Roger. 'If you can take him off my hands for an hour or two,' she said, 'I shall be forever indebted to you.'

II

And so it was arranged. The rendezvous was a well-known restaurant in the West End, Roger exercised his uncanny knack of finding a parking place, the table that Stephen had booked for two was changed to one for four, and they were all well settled down before Sally arrived. She was a very pretty girl with fair curly hair and was wearing a severely cut suit which somehow looked incongruous on her. But it was the fluffiness of her appearance that was deceptive, not her attire. A very few minutes conversation served to convince both Antony and Roger that this was a young lady on whom there were no flies at all.

Stephen effected the introductions, displaying a simple and rather touching pride in the girl's attractiveness. 'They're asking questions about Veronica,' he said then. 'You remember what Dad told us the other night?'

'Last night,' said Sally. 'Yes, I remember very well.' She

134

eyed Antony reflectively for a moment. 'And, of course, I knew all about Mr Maitland before that.'

This rather sweeping statement was calculated to put Antony in a bad mood for the rest of the day, and Roger was relieved when he said lightly, as though trying to inject a less serious note into the conversation, 'Not all, I hope, Miss Hargreaves.'

She neither retracted the statement nor modified it. 'The man who always wins his cases,' she said, but this time she smiled and her tone was as light as his had been.

'I wish that were true.'

'And now you're worried about Veronica's sister,' said Sally, who obviously had a passion for getting everything completely straight in her mind. 'First because you don't want her to be under any illusion about the kind of things Veronica was capable of, and secondly because she may herself be accused of causing Veronica's death.'

'That's near enough,' Antony began, but Stephen didn't allow him to finish but broke in eagerly.

'I've had a perfectly marvellous idea about that, Sally. Supposing Veronica did it again, and it's Fran who died at the Chelsea flat, not her.'

Sally looked a little doubtful. 'I'm supposing it,' she said, 'but it doesn't sound very likely. What would her motive be?'

'If Veronica is dead she can't be brought to trial for murdering grandfather.'

'No,' said Sally still doubtfully. 'But from what Mr Maitland says it seems the surviving sister may be charged with murder anyway.'

'That's only because the police didn't accept the death as suicide. Of course if they're wrong about that it invalidates my whole argument,' Stephen conceded. 'All the same –'

'But someone would have known,' Sally protested. 'Were they really as alike as all that? I know Veronica said they were identical twins, but –'

135

'As far as anyone could see they really were identical,' said Antony. 'There may be some distinguishing marks on their bodies, but unless either of them had occasion to consult a doctor lately it isn't likely that anyone but themselves knows about them. And the police, quite reasonably, accepted Fran Procter's identification of her sister.'

'Well, on second thoughts, I think this idea of Stephen's is a pretty good one,' said Sally, 'and surely the police could go back to the doctor who knew them as children and ask him.'

'It isn't only appearance,' said Roger. 'From what I'm told their personalities were quite different, and the one who calls herself Fran now is nothing like Veronica. Isn't that so, Antony?'

'That's certainly true, and Johnny Lund, who was Veronica's solicitor and now is Fran's, had met Fran once, though rather briefly. He's in no doubt that it's she who is still alive.'

'All the same,' said Sally stubbornly, 'I think the police should be told. There must be someone who would know if either of them had a birthmark. Veronica lived in the nurses' hostel when she was training at St Walburga's for instance, she might have had a room-mate.' She turned to Roger then. 'Are you an associate of Mr Maitland's?' she asked in a friendly way.

If Stephen hadn't known perfectly well who he was Roger would have answered this in the affirmative, as he'd had occasion to do many times in the past. As it was, 'Merely a friend,' he said. 'I offered to drive him out to Wimbledon, and as I'm acquainted with Mrs Keats Antony thought my presence while they were talking might put her at her ease.'

'Isabel nervous? What nonsense,' said Sally robustly. 'If ever anyone was capable of looking after themselves she is. And I mean that in the nicest sort of way,' she added reassuringly to Stephen. 'You know I can't bear weaklings.'

'Well, there was no need for nervousness anyway,' Antony assured her, 'as my questions were solely concerned with

136

Veronica Procter. But there are a good many people who get the jitters at the mere mention of anything concerned with the law, and for all I knew Mrs Keats might have been one of them.'

'If I know her,' said Sally smiling, 'she talked a blue streak and told you nothing at all.'

'On the contrary, I found what she told me very helpful indeed.'

'Did you? Well I'm afraid you won't be able to say the same about me. I quite agree that Fran – if she is the survivor – should be made to face up to what her sister did, but I was only at the house once while old Mr Keats was ill, and Veronica wasn't at dinner with us that night. In fact I didn't see her at all.'

At this point the waiter returned, obviously expecting that they had already studied their menus and were ready to order. To pacify him they ordered drinks, and when these arrived with commendable speed went on with their talk with the menus still ignored beside them. 'Obviously I didn't think you could help me in the question of old Mr Keats's death,' said Antony. 'With your fiancé away I didn't even know if you had been at the house or not.'

'Oh, Isabel approves of me,' said Sally. 'In fact I think she's been trying to get Stephen to the point of proposing for years, but in the meantime she's always treated me as if we were already engaged.'

'And weren't you?' Maitland wasn't very interested in Stephen Keats's love life, but some comment seemed to be called for. And as he spoke he remembered the rather disparaging remarks Veronica had made about this pleasant-seeming girl, who had apparently done her best to befriend her.

'Not until he came home this time,' said Sally. 'I think,' she added in a confidential tone, 'that he found he missed me more than he expected. Well, that won't have to happen again, Sir George will have a fit but I mean to give up my job and go with him, it wouldn't seem like a proper marriage otherwise, and I'm not afraid of – of primitive conditions.'

'No reason why you should be, darling,' Stephen assured her. 'But let's get this business of Mr Maitland's over, then we can have our lunch in peace. He knows we took Veronica out with us sometimes, and we were both wondering whether perhaps she'd been a little more confiding with you than she was with me. Whether you know anything about her other friends.'

'Or where she went on her days off,' Antony added.

'I'm afraid I can't help you either. I'm not saying I'd have chosen Veronica as a companion, especially when it meant making up a threesome, but she was quite amusing to be with and there was always plenty to talk about.'

'What kind of things?'

'Not personal, if that's what you're hoping. It's rather strange looking back, but all I learned about her was that she had a twin sister who was trying to be an artist and lived in Chelsea. I didn't get the impression that she visited Fran very often though. We'd talk about current affairs, books, films we'd seen . . . but I don't think that she ever went to the cinema except with us, or with Julian and Jean. And she was very conscientious about getting back to the house in time to get Mr Keats to bed. And now,' she said, picking up her menu at last, 'I think we'd better get on with our meal, because I'm still a working woman even if Stephen is a gentleman of leisure for another few weeks.'

III

So Antony got back to chambers, and Roger to the City, in reasonably good time. Which was just as well from Maitland's point of view because he was greeted by Willett, who popped out of the clerk's office like a jack-in-the-box, to announce that Mr Lund wanted him urgently. The telephone number Johnny had left was vaguely familiar, and when he dialled it it was Fran's voice that answered.

'Johnny's here,' she said, 'if you want him. I called him because the police are coming again, and he seems to think you ought to know.'

'Don't bother to put him on then,' said Antony. 'I'll come over right away.' And rang off without waiting for her to question him.

His taxi drew up in the narrow lane outside the house where Fran lived, just behind a police car. Except for the driver the occupants emerged while he was paying off his cab, and he stood staring for a moment before going across to meet them. Sykes and Mayhew he had expected, though he had found it a little surprising that Mayhew had been sitting at the front beside the uniformed driver. It was the sight of the third man that both astonished and alarmed him. 'I don't believe it!' he said flatly, coming up with them.

The third man turned to look at him. 'I, on the other hand, was expecting to see you here, Mr Maitland,' he said. 'But what don't you believe?'

'Detective Chief Superintendents don't make house calls,' said Antony. 'Unless perhaps the Prime Minister's been murdered or something like that. Perhaps it's as well I am here,' he added looking from one to the other of them. 'If the Yard thinks it's essential to send three' – he paused deliberately before he went on – 'three large men to intimidate one medium-sized girl, perhaps she needs all the witnesses she can get to see fair play.'

'That, Mr Maitland, is a most unnecessary remark as you well know,' said Chief Superintendent Briggs heavily. He was a big, burly man with a ruddy complexion, and with hair that had receded so far from a bulging forehead that now it formed no more than a rather untidy fringe around his bald pate. His

139

relationship with Maitland was an odd one. They disliked each other intensely, and had done since the beginning of their acquaintance many years before; but whereas the detective quite simply distrusted counsel and believed him capable of any sort of double dealing, Antony – though he had been known to refer to the other man as a pig-headed old bastard – had never suspected him of anything worse than a tendency to make up his mind very firmly in what was sometimes a wrong-headed way. 'There is no question of intimidation,' Briggs was going on, 'but there are certain circumstances about this case –'

'I think perhaps any explanation can wait until we are indoors.' That was Sykes in his role of peacemaker, a part he fell into automatically when these two came face to face. 'Miss Procter is expecting us,' he added by way of inducement. Detective Inspector Mayhew was already ringing the bell.

Johnny Lund let them in, and raised a startled eyebrow in Antony's direction when Briggs surged forward and announced his own name and rank without waiting for a more formal introduction. 'Let's get upstairs, Johnny,' said Antony encouragingly. 'Then perhaps we shall find out what this is all about.'

Recently Fran Procter's tiny sitting-room had been doing more duty than it was designed for. Briggs's presence seemed to reduce its size still further. Fran's eyes widened a little at the sight of a man she didn't know, but even when Maitland took it upon himself to introduce the Chief Superintendent she had obviously no idea that there was anything particularly strange about his being there.

'If you want to look at the desk,' she said, 'it's over there. But you said, Mr Sykes, that your men had quite finished examining it,' she added ingenuously, 'so Johnny was kind enough to put some hinges on. Just temporarily, until I can get it to an antique dealer. It looked so awful with the flap hanging down like that, not to mention the fact that it showed

140

how untidily I usually keep all my papers.'

'That's quite in order, Miss Procter,' said Sykes reassuringly. 'This visit, I'm afraid, is only in part due to what happened last night. But first perhaps it would be more comfortable if we all sat down.'

'Oh yes, of course, I'm sorry.' She went immediately to a chair, and waved a sort of general invitation to the others to follow her example. There were five easy chairs in the room, and Johnny disappeared for a moment and returned with a wooden one that was obviously from the kitchen. Just for a moment amusement took precedence over any other emotion in Maitland's mind. Seated around like this it looked such an intimate gathering, but he recalled his thoughts sternly after no more than a moment. There was nothing funny about Briggs's presence here.

And indeed almost immediately his worst fears were confirmed. Inspector Mayhew, like Sykes, spoke gently to the girl, and Antony was quite sure that his and Johnny's presence had nothing to do with that, but what he was saying wasn't quite so reassuring. 'There are a few questions, Miss Procter, that the Chief Superintendent would like to ask you himself. But before we start I must warn you . . .'

Antony felt Johnny's eyes turn on him in quick alarm and shook his head slightly in an admonitory way. He had a feeling that any objecting there was to be done had better be done by himself. At least, he hoped, he could keep a clear head as far as Fran's predicament was concerned. Whereas Johnny . . .

'I don't quite understand,' said Fran, 'but of course I'll tell you anything you want to know.' She turned a little to face Briggs directly, and gave him a confiding smile.

'Perhaps you would tell us, Miss Procter, exactly what happened the evening your sister died,' he said, obviously unmoved by her friendliness.

'But that'll be the third time! I told the detective who came first, and I told these two gentlemen. There's really nothing to add.'

'All the same I should like to hear it for myself.' The coldness in Briggs's voice contrasted oddly with her own more open manner.

'Very well.' As far as Antony could remember her statement was almost word for word what it had been before. When she had finished Briggs leaned forward a little, as though the better to emphasize his next remarks.

'About this phone call you say your sister received –'

'She was talking on the phone when I came back into the room, I don't know whether she made the call or somebody rang her. I wouldn't have heard the bell when I was down by the front door.'

'That is really immaterial. The only evidence besides your own that this conversation ever took place would have been your sister's, and she can no longer tell us.'

'Well, of course she can't. She was speaking to a man, I told you that, because she said "he" was coming when she told me to go out.'

'I'm sure you will forgive me for saying, Miss Procter, that part of the story seems a little strange to me. This, after all, is your home, isn't it? Would even your sister order you from it so peremptorily?'

'Did you ever meet Miss Veronica Procter, Chief Superintendent?' Antony asked, judging it time to make his presence felt. 'Knowing her disposition, and Miss Frances Procter's obliging nature, there is nothing at all to wonder about in that.'

'That, Mr Maitland, is exactly what I should have expected you to say.' The veneer of politeness deserted Briggs altogether when he spoke to Antony. 'Now, Miss Procter, I think we should both disregard the interruption and perhaps you will tell me whether you went alone to the cinema, and whether you met anyone you knew while you were out.'

'I was alone and I met nobody.' The first touches of alarm were evident in Fran's voice. 'But I assure you I went to see

142

that film I've described, I went that very night. But the Paris Cinema usually runs its features for quite a while, sometimes as long as a month, so there's no way I can prove I hadn't seen it before.'

'That is also something that seems irrelevant,' said Briggs. 'Death by arsenic poisoning is not – shall we say? – the most enlivening spectacle. I hardly think you would have wished to stay here and watch your sister die.'

Maitland broke in quickly. 'You see how ready Miss Procter is to answer your question, Chief Superintendent. Are you now accusing her of having brought about her sister's death?'

Briggs turned very deliberately and looked at him. 'Surely a man of your intelligence must realise that that's exactly what I'm doing,' he said.

'Don't sneer, Chief Superintendent, it doesn't become you,' said Maitland. 'In that case, Fran, I think we won't answer any more of the police's questions. You have of course no obligation to do so, the next move is up to them.'

'What about last night?' said Johnny, suddenly coming to life. 'Surely it's obvious that whoever killed Veronica came back to look for something, and hit out at Fran when she disturbed him.'

'Not a very severe injury,' said Briggs. 'It may interest you to know, Mr Lund, that we called on the doctor who attended your client before we came here today.'

'Well, he could confirm what I say. And as for it not being a serious injury, she must have been unconscious for nearly an hour when I found her.'

'There are two answers to that, Mr Lund, but meanwhile let me tell you what the doctor had to say. It would require a certain degree of desperation, but the blow could have been self-inflicted. If that were the case, can you swear that Miss Frances Procter was actually unconscious when you found her?'

'Of course she was!'

'Can you swear that?'

'I thought she was dead, that's how sure I was. When I carried her into the bedroom there wasn't a sign of consciousness at all.'

'Then we may go on to our next hypothesis. Some other party, somebody say as concerned as you are, Mr Lund, for her well-being, might have co-operated in this whole rather stupid plan to exonerate her.'

'But I –'

'Be quiet, Johnny!' said Maitland sharply. 'You're quite right, Chief Superintendent, in saying it would have been a stupid plan. It was quite obvious how the police would regard it. Your being here proves that.'

'Not so obvious to Mr Lund perhaps, since he brought the subject up himself just now.'

'Are you accusing him of – of faking evidence to get his client off?'

'I have made no accusation on that score as yet.'

'Ah, yes, there's a little matter of p-proof, isn't there?' As all the men present knew, though Fran could not, the slight stammer was the first sign that his temper was very precariously held indeed.

'Exactly. But you can see now why I felt my presence was desirable this afternoon, Mr Maitland. Where an officer of the court is suspected of conspiring with his instructing solicitor to . . . to fake evidence was your word, wasn't it? You can quite see that the whole affair takes on a much more serious aspect.'

'Heaven and earth!' said Antony blankly. In spite of his uncle's warning the implications of this came as a surprise as well as a shock to him. 'Am I supposed to be in this as w-well?'

'I make no accusation,' said Briggs again. 'You spoke of proof, Mr Maitland, and legal proof I admit I do not have. But I'm entitled to my own opinion, and my knowledge of your

144

activities through the years convinces me –'

'You're entitled to y-your own opinion,' said Antony, 's-so long as you k-keep it to yourself.'

Briggs was suddenly on his feet. 'Are you by any chance threatening me?' he asked angrily.

When their superior officer had risen Sykes and Mayhew had followed his example, perhaps with some idea that restraint might be necessary. Maitland looked from one to the other of them, and unexpectedly he laughed with something that sounded like real amusement and came leisurely to his feet in his turn.

'No, I'm not threatening you,' he said. For the moment he had himself in hand and all trace of the stammer had gone. 'Though an action for slander might be amusing, of course – that's what you meant, isn't it? – especially as your own people would have to give evidence on my behalf. But quite frankly neither Mr Lund nor myself takes your allegations seriously enough to be bothered with such a course.'

'You're afraid of what might come out,' Briggs asserted.

'No.' Maitland let the single word lie between them for a moment while the silence lengthened. 'I'm sorry to disappoint you, Chief Superintendent,' he said then. 'Conspiracy to d-defeat the ends of justice sounds very well, but since nothing of that nature took p-place nothing can possibly be proved, so the defence of truth wouldn't be open to you. Besides,' he added in as gentle a tone as his uncle might have used, 'I never for a m-moment thought that what happened to Miss Procter here would convince you of her innocence, as my uncle could tell you. We talked the matter over l-late last night.'

There was no doubt about it now, Briggs was furiously angry. 'Of course, Sir Nicholas would back you up in any story you like to tell,' he said.

'Do you really think so?' Antony managed a hopeful note in his voice. 'But then,' he added sighing, 'you don't know him very well, do you?'

145

For the moment Briggs seemed to be speechless and Sykes intervened in his placid way. 'This may all seem very amusing to you, Mr Maitland, but perhaps you'll take it more seriously when I tell you that Inspector Mayhew has a warrant in his pocket for Miss Procter's arrest.'

Antony swung round to him. 'On what charge?' he demanded. Sykes knew as well as he did that his temper was lost irretrievably, but–perhaps as the detective had intended–his quiet tones had a steadying effect.

'A rather more serious one than obstructing the police. She will be charged with poisoning her sister.'

Maitland turned quickly towards the chair where Fran was still sitting. 'Do you understand, Fran?' She nodded dumbly. 'You have to go with Inspector Mayhew now, but you mustn't answer any more questions. There will be a magistrate's court hearing in the morning but you won't be called to give evidence. So . . . no more statements until the trial comes on.'

'Tomorrow morning–?'

'Mr Lund and I will be there and we'll see you before the hearing. Meanwhile you've nothing whatever to worry about . . . just remember that.'

'I'll try to. Can I take anything with me . . . some toilet things and something for overnight.'

'I'll phone my wife and get her to come over and pack what she thinks you'll need, and Mr Lund will bring them to you. Or perhaps–' He broke off there; he had just realised that Meg, living so near, could probably do that small chore just as well, but there was no point in saying so. 'When Johnny and I have just had a look at the warrant–'

Mayhew was already holding it out. 'Very well,' said Maitland, reading the document quickly and handing it back.

'I could go at least as far as the police station,' Johnny suggested.

'No, I want you here.' Maitland's tone was suddenly very decided. 'Besides, since I don't expect you all intend to squash

146

into the same car going back, I imagine we may have the pleasure of these gentlemen's presence for a little longer,' he said, dividing a glance between Briggs and Sykes.

'If you wish it certainly, Mr Maitland,' said Sykes quietly.

'If it's not asking too much of you.' He waited until Johnny had found Fran's coat (really he seemed to be making himself very much at home here already) and announced his intention of going down to the front door with her and the Inspector. As Lund's voice, still adjuring her not to worry, faded gradually from their hearing Antony turned to the two senior detectives. 'I notice that the warrant was made out in the name of Frances Procter,' he said.

Briggs found his voice. 'Of course it was,' he snapped.

'I heard an interesting suggestion today,' said Antony. Only Sykes, who understood him fairly well, realised that his anger had gone far deeper than the stammering stage that usually marked it, and had become cold and deadly and might prove dangerous, whether to himself or to its object there was just no telling. 'It was to the effect that the body of the girl who was found dead in this flat was identified only by her sister. Her identical twin sister. As Veronica Procter was suspected of having murdered her employer, she might well have wished to disappear into another identity. It would be amusing – wouldn't it? – if Mr Lund and I got your prisoner off on a technicality.'

'If there's any doubt about the identification,' said Briggs, falling headlong into the trap, 'Veronica Procter lived with the Keats family for nearly three years and one of them could provide corroboration.'

'Yes, but in the circumstances could any of them be positive? I really think you should think about that, Chief Inspector,' he added to Sykes.

Sykes only smiled and shook his head at him. Briggs said heatedly, 'Am I to understand that you intend to appear in this case yourself?'

147

'Of course I do, why shouldn't I?'

'I warn you, Mr Maitland—'

This time Sykes interrupted without ceremony. 'If you're handling the case when it comes to trial, allegations may be made in court which, though they couldn't be proved, might be embarrassing to you.'

'Thank you, Chief Inspector,' said Antony politely. But suddenly his temper ran away with him again, and he said far more than he had intended. 'If you must know, both of you, I've no intention of letting the case get to trial,' he said. 'That child wouldn't hurt a fly and I mean to prove it.'

At this point Sykes, probably fearing apoplexy, succeeded in persuading Briggs to leave. He looked back reproachfully at Antony as he followed his superior officer out of the door, but made no more open comment. Not that one was necessary, Maitland knew well enough what he was thinking.

Johnny had come back into the room a few minutes before, and as soon as they were alone he demanded forcefully, 'Why did you want to put that idea into their heads. We might have sprung it on them at the trial.'

'Believe me, Johnny, it was quite irresistible,' Maitland told him. 'If we'd tried that the prosecution would just have asked for an adjournment and by the time they'd rustled up the family doctor we'd have been no better off. Besides, Sykes didn't believe it for a moment, and neither will Briggs once he's recovered his temper. And I'm as sure as you are that it's Fran they've arrested. If it weren't for anything else your own feelings—'

'Are they as obvious as all that?' asked Johnny, making no attempt at denial.

'Yes, they are. You didn't even like Veronica, but you've fallen for Fran like a ton of bricks. It's that fact and the fact that you found her that made the police suspect some funny business about what happened last night.'

'Do you think we ought to hand the case over? I wouldn't

148

want to prejudice her defence in any way.'

'No, I don't,' said Maitland positively.

'I heard what you said about clearing it up before it came to trial,' said Johnny, 'but –'

'Yes, I know that was rash of me,' Antony admitted. 'If we can't manage that between us we may have to call in someone else. But what I wanted to ask you, Johnny, is, where were you last night before you came to see Fran?'

'I got a meal early when I left the office, meaning to come round straight away and tell her what you'd told me about your talk with Maurice Keats. Since you know so much you may as well know this too, it was only an excuse to see her again. But then I couldn't get my nerve up. I walked round for a couple of hours before I finally finished up here. I haven't got an alibi, if that's what you mean.'

'No, it's a pity, but it can't be helped. She's a nice girl, Johnny, and I think she likes you too.'

'And a fat lot of good that will do,' said Johnny despondently, 'when I tell her about Dad.'

'I have a feeling . . . but never mind that now. I'd better get on the phone to see about getting a bag packed for Fran. I thought,' he added as he walked over to the telephone, 'that perhaps Meg would do it. It'll save time as she lives so near.'

IV

That evening when Maitland got home the study door was shut, and though Gibbs was hovering at the back of the hall as usual it was without any words for him other than a grudging 'Good Evening'. In spite of that Antony went across to the study, if he went straight upstairs, as he was longing to do, Jenny would only tell him that Uncle Nick hated to be kept in

149

the dark. Sir Nicholas and Vera were alone together this evening and from the stiff way he held himself they both concluded immediately that he had had a harrowing day and that, as seemed to happen when he was over-tired, his shoulder was giving him more pain than usual. Sir Nicholas immediately offered sherry, but Antony shook his head.

'I think I'll wait and have one with Jenny,' he said. 'She's likely to need reviving too when I tell her what's been going on today.'

'What has been going on?' asked Sir Nicholas suspiciously.

'Briggs is on the warpath.'

'We knew that already.'

'Yes, you warned me, but I didn't take you seriously. I'd better tell you first of all that Fran Procter has been arrested. As I guessed, the police idea is that the crack on the head she got may have been self-inflicted, though they admit that would have required some determination. A more likely explanation, they feel, is that someone else did it at her request, or at any rate with her agreement. Briggs was there.'

'You mean at her flat when they arrested her?' asked Sir Nicholas incredulously.

'That's exactly what I do mean.'

'But surely –'

'Yes, that's what I said too, Uncle Nick. His answer was that where the accused's lawyers have connived with her in an attempt to prove her innocence it was a serious matter with which he thought it was his duty to associate himself.'

'Good God,' said Sir Nicholas blankly. 'So this is supposed to have been an idea of yours and Johnny's? I know what I said, but I didn't think the accusation would be made outright.'

'Well, it was. I think Johnny is supposed to have carried it out, after all he found her and there's no evidence except his that she was unconscious at that time. He can't prove the time of his arrival either, because he was wandering about trying to

150

get up courage to go and see her. It's a stupid idea, because however much she'd begged him to help her I'm quite sure he couldn't have brought himself to hurt her in any way.'

Neither of his listeners was lured by this interesting byway. 'No proof of any of this,' said Vera flatly, entering the conversation for the first time.

'Of course not, nor can there be. All the same Briggs warned us against continuing to act for Fran. He said allegations might be made in court that would prove embarrassing to us even in the absence of proof. No, that last bit was Sykes, but it comes to the same thing.'

'Are you going to take his advice?' asked Sir Nicholas.

'It all depends.'

'What is that supposed to mean?' His tone was colder now.

'I lost my temper,' Antony admitted.

'Again?' said Sir Nicholas resignedly.

'I'm afraid so, but if you'd heard him, Uncle Nick –'

'I am, for my sins, only too well acquainted with Chief Superintendent Briggs.'

'I've a feeling you mean for *my* sins,' said Antony. 'Anyway, I told him the case would never come to trial, because I'd prove him wrong before there was a chance of that.'

'Thereby reinforcing his suspicions,' Sir Nicholas pointed out.

'Yes, I suppose so. I hadn't thought of it exactly in that light,' said Antony. 'There's nothing else to tell you really, except that I shan't be in chambers in the morning. There's the magistrate's court hearing and I want to talk to Fran first.'

When he had gone Vera looked across at her husband. 'Nice mess,' she said. 'If you ask him he might give up criminal practice.'

Sir Nicholas's smile rivalled his wife's for grimness. 'Do you really think so, my dear? For one thing he still thinks we're exaggerating what Briggs may be capable of. For another, even if he agreed with me, the first hard luck story that came his way would change his mind.'

'Suppose it would,' said Vera. 'Always knew it really. Not the sort of person to pass by on the other side.'

'You wouldn't want him to be,' asserted Sir Nicholas. 'Any more than I would. Though I sometimes wish,' he added, 'that he hadn't been endowed with quite such a knack of raising the devil.'

V

To his surprise when he got upstairs he found Roger and Meg with Jenny. 'What on earth are you two doing here?' he demanded, glancing in a marked manner at his watch. 'If Jenny's going to feed you before the theatre, Meg, something had better be done about it.'

'They're staying to dinner . . . at the usual time,' said Jenny. 'Isn't that nice? At least, not so nice for Meg, because she has laryngitis, she couldn't possibly make herself heard in the theatre.'

'I'm sorry about that Meg. You sounded all right when we spoke, or I wouldn't have bothered you to do that chore for me.'

'It's got worse since then,' said Meg, her voice a hoarse whisper. 'Anyway, darling, it didn't matter. I feel perfectly all right.'

'Well, by the time she rang me up she just croaked at me over the phone,' said Jenny. 'And of course I said, come to dinner. It's not often we get a chance like this on a weekday.'

'All too rarely,' said Roger. Probably he meant to say that lightly, but it came out with great feeling.

'Never mind, darling,' said Meg. It might be more accurate

to say croaked, as Jenny had done. 'I've quite made up my mind to take some time off in the summer as you suggested. After all it's only fair to Stella.' It sounded as though talking might be a pretty painful business, but obviously she wasn't going to let that hinder her from taking a fair share in the conversation.

'Well, I'm sorry about the throat but I'm glad to see you,' said Antony. He sank down into the wing chair that he usually used when he wasn't feeling too restless to sit still. 'It will save me telling the story of this afternoon a third time, Roger, because as you may be my life-line in this business you'll have to know about it.'

Jenny was at the writing-table pouring a glass of sherry for her husband, but she looked round at that. 'Something dangerous?' she said.

'Not in the way you mean, love.' She gave him a suspicious look and then went back to her task. When she had placed the sherry on the table at his elbow he went on to recount his talk with Briggs.

'Uncle Nick would say that was worse than–than physical danger,' said Jenny. 'Have you told him?'

'Yes, I've heeded the counsel you've always given me not to keep things from him. I don't say he was actually cheered by the news, but for once he didn't get as far as blaming me for the whole thing. Only, you see, I've more or less burned my boats by what I said to Briggs. What he believes or doesn't believe doesn't matter, not to me at any rate. Only–'

'It's a pity you can't send him a challenge,' said Meg. 'Pistols for two and coffee for one. Wouldn't that be a lovely way of settling it?'

'I'm afraid if trial by combat was still in fashion it would be Counsel for the Prosecution I should have to fight,' said Antony lightly. 'There are one or two I wouldn't mind putting a hole through,' he added thoughtfully, 'but it would be just my luck to come up against someone like Kevin O'Brien, who's probably a crack shot, and whom anyway I don't want to kill. So I think we'd better just stick to the usual wearying business of question and answer.'

'That's where I come in?' Roger inquired.

'Yes, and for the same reason I asked you to come with me this morning. I'm only suspected of being the brains behind the plot to clear Fran Procter by half killing her, but Johnny's suspected of having actually done the dirty work. So what I need is somebody completely unbiased. Besides there's no doubt at all,' he added smiling, 'that in the eyes of Mrs Blythe Keats at least – she's a fashion consultant – your sartorial splendour will make a good impression.' (As Roger had changed for the evening into a pair of old slacks and a pullover anyone who didn't know him during working hours would have thought this rather an odd remark.)

'He can't help it, darling, it's part of his stock-in-trade,' Meg assured him, 'Whoever would think of entrusting his affairs to an indigent-looking stockbroker?'

'You shouldn't try to talk, Meg,' said Jenny. 'I'm sure it hurts.'

She received a rather impish grin in reply. 'Not so much as keeping quiet would do, darling,' Meg told her.

'Anyway,' said Roger, 'sartorial splendour or not, it was all very well taking me with you this morning, and I'll admit you thought up a pretty good excuse for doing that. But with the rest of the family . . . I can hardly present myself at the offices of Keats & Company and expect them to believe I'm there to give them a little more confidence.'

'I've seen Maurice Keats already, alone,' said Antony. 'But I very much want to see Julian, and I shouldn't object to bumping into Maurice again, accidental-like. But if I go alone . . . can't you think of some business that would take you round to their place, Roger? Then we could encounter one another quite casually in the reception room, and perhaps arrange for the whole conversation to be held on quite an informal level.'

'I can certainly think of something,' said Roger obligingly. 'When do you want this chance encounter to take place?'

'It would have to be in the afternoon if it's tomorrow, can you manage that? There's the magistrate's court hearing in the morning and I'm not quite sure how long that will hold me up.'

'All right then, give me a call when you're free. That still doesn't take care of this fashion consultant person with the unlikely name. I mean, they're only talking to you because they think you want to know about Veronica Procter's friends, the faintest hint that you want a witness to what they say—'

'Yes, I know it makes life difficult. However, I think when we go to see Mrs Ralph Keats, and her assistant Jean Ingelow at the same time with any luck—did I tell you she's Julian Keats's girl-friend?—I shall just dither a little, and show all the symptoms of someone embarrassed to find himself in a purely female establishment. They'll laugh about it after we've gone, but they won't think it particularly odd that *I* feel the need of a bodyguard.'

'I don't know,' said Roger doubtfully. 'What do fashion consultants do anyway?'

'I'm not quite sure. Meg would know, wouldn't she? You can write it down if it hurts to talk,' Antony added kindly as he turned to her.

Meg didn't take advantage of this invitation. 'Jenny's my fashion consultant,' she said.

'She doesn't design the things you wear on stage.'

'No, of course not, darling.' Her enforced silence or near silence, was obviously trying Meg's patience a good deal. 'Do you remember, Jenny, all those years ago when we hardly knew each other, your making me buy a hat with a cluster of marguerites, and how cross you were when someone said they were dog daisies?'

'I remember,' said Antony before his wife could speak.

155

'And I also remember a perfectly dreadful coat with rabbit fur round the collar, that you wouldn't get rid of at any price because it was warm.'

Well, I was right about that, wasn't I? And if you want to know about fashion designers, darling, I don't usually have much to do with that side of a production, except to scream with agony if they try to put me into a dress I don't like. But mostly we use consultants when it's a question of dressing a period play. Ossie's pretty faithful to his own designer, but sometimes he needs a little help.'

'Well, is the suggestion I made reasonable?'

'You can do it, darling, I know that perfectly well. But if you're envisaging something like a permanent fashion show I don't think that's what you'll find. A very untidy office, unless this Mrs Keats is an absolute martinet, and a lot of drawing-boards. And if you're thinking all the people who work for her will be women, I wouldn't mind betting you'll be wrong.'

By the time she'd finished this her voice had almost faded completely. 'Poor Meg.' Antony smiled at her. 'I think I'll do it my way in any case, after all she isn't to know I have inside information.'

At this point Jenny said something about dishing up and set off purposefully for the kitchen, Roger followed her, as he so often did when there was a tray that might need carrying, so natural and customary an act that neither of the other two thought to question it. But Roger had been watching Jenny's face while they were talking, and had something else in mind.

He found her peering into a pan of boiling potatoes, and prodding them gingerly with a fork. 'They're done,' she said without looking round.

'Then I'll drain them for you. They look nice and floury,' he said a moment later, when the potatoes were steaming in the colander, and it was only then that he turned to look at her searchingly. 'You're not really worried about physical danger, are you, Jenny?'

156

She didn't answer that directly. 'Do you think it's very foolish of me?' she asked.

'In this case I'm sure –'

'Roger, don't you see, in a case like this . . . two people have been murdered and one attacked? If someone thinks Antony's getting near the truth–' She took a vegetable dish from the warming oven and transferred the potatoes to it not bothering to complete a sentence to which she was perfectly well aware her companion knew the ending. 'If you could be around as much as possible in the next few days,' she added, looking up at him pleadingly.

'I'll be around,' said Roger lightly.

'And will you try to persuade him to be careful?'

'Jenny, that would come much better from you.'

'No, because of a sort of vow I made years ago that I'd never try to hold him back from anything he felt he ought to do. It was only to myself of course, but still . . . of all our friends, Roger, you're the only one he's willing to talk to openly. I don't quite know why.'

Somebody else might have replied lightly, 'My natural charm of manner,' and killed the conversation dead in its tracks.Roger said seriously, 'It's because he once had to admit to me, at least by implication, that there are things he can't do . . . physically, I mean.'

'His shoulder,' said Jenny sadly.

'Precisely . . . as he himself would say, and be ticked off by Meg for getting like Uncle Nick. But I suppose once the ice was broken–' He paused, thinking about that, and then suddenly began to laugh, leaning forward to take her hand, inviting her to join him. 'It was almost literally that, Jenny,' he said. 'Into the river, fully clothed, on a beastly cold evening. Do you remember?'

'But Antony can swim, after a fashion.'

'It was getting over the side of the *Susannah* that was the trouble. But never mind that now. What maggot has he got into his head this time?'

'Just that Fran Procter is innocent, and I daresay he's right about that. But I wish he hadn't said . . . what he did . . . to Superintendent Briggs.'

'He says it was because he lost his temper.'

'Yes, but I think it was more than that, I think he's got some idea into his head as to who might be responsible. I don't understand it, Roger, the whole thing seems a muddle to me.'

'The first death, after all,' said Roger, harking back to what she had said a moment before, 'was caused by Veronica Procter. Or doesn't Antony agree with that either?'

'I don't know what he thinks.'

'Never mind, Jenny, between us I think we can see no harm's done. If you must worry you'd be far more sensible to do so about Briggs's attitude.'

'That's what Uncle Nick would say, and I do of course,' Jenny admitted. 'All the same –' She broke off and stood looking at him, her grey eyes worried. 'I've broken my vow anyway, haven't I?' she asked. 'I mean *I'm* not going to say anything to Antony but I've asked you to do it for me.'

'Don't even think about it,' Roger advised her. 'All you've really done is to tell me you're worried, and you ought to know me well enough by now to realise that the result would be the same whether you added anything to that or not.'

'Yes, I suppose so,' said Jenny more cheerfully. 'Anyway I feel better just for talking. And the roast will be burned to a cinder if we don't take it out of the oven. I think we shall need the biggest tray, Roger.'

A good deal later when dinner had been eaten, the remnants cleared away, and they were all gathered round the fire again, it was Meg who reverted to the subject. 'Something you said made me wonder if Johnny's done it again,' she remarked.

'If you mean falling in love, I'm pretty sure of it. Not that I think he'll ever get up the nerve to tell her, after what

158

happened with Lynn.'

'Don't you see, darling, this one's the ideal girl for him? I don't think any of us is really in any doubt that her sister is a murderer, so she can't possibly object to the things Johnny's father did.'

'That,' said Antony, 'is the last thing in the world I want pointed out to him. No really, Meg,' he added when he saw her mutinous look, 'I've been at great pains not to let him know what I think happened to old Mr Keats.'

'But why ever not, darling?'

'Because, *darling*,' said Antony, echoing the word with a rather savage intonation, 'he'll never get his nerve back if he thinks she's accepted him for that reason.'

'But if he won't tell her –'

'I'll see that he does. Or rather,' he added as an idea suddenly struck him, 'I think that might be a job for you and Jenny. Women have much more devious minds than men . . . don't you think?'

Thursday, May 2nd

I

The talk with Fran Procter next morning before the magistrate's court hearing was a brief one. She repeated her story of what had happened the night her sister died, but a plea of Not Guilty had been a foregone conclusion anyway. No hope of proving that what she said was true, and even if it were possible it wouldn't help, the poison might well have been administered before she left the flat. As for the telephone call and the visitor Veronica expected, there was no proof of either, just as Fran might insist that she didn't want the legacy anyway and both statements would be put down to diversionary tactics now that she'd got scared of the consequences of what she'd done. The blow she had received on the head came under that category too. Their best hope was that she would prove a believable witness when the trial came on.

All the same Antony would dearly have liked to ask Chief Inspector Sykes whether, if it had been left to him, he would have gone ahead with the arrest at this point. Maitland had a nasty feeling that Briggs wouldn't mind at all if the girl got off, provided her counsel could be implicated in some sort of trickery, to the extent at least of damaging his reputation.

'The trial won't come on for several weeks,' he told her as a result of these cogitations. 'Probably not until the Trinity term – that is June or even July. So the best thing you can do in the meantime is to keep a clear head, and try to prepare yourself mentally for what I'm afraid will be a very unpleasant

160

experience.'

'That's all very well, Mr Maitland, but what about you and Mr Lund? That horrible man yesterday –'

'He made some accusations that he couldn't possibly substantiate. Nothing for you to worry about.'

'He seemed to hate you.'

'I think as far as his feelings for me are concerned that's probably right.'

'But Mr Lund told me before you arrived that you said you'd never let the case come to trial.'

'I'm afraid that was said in anger. If I've raised your hopes unduly I'm sorry for it.'

'And Veronica?' said Fran rather desolately.

It was Johnny who answered. 'If we can find out who killed your sister, I think it follows that we should find out at the same time who killed poor Mr Keats.'

'Do you think so? Do you really think so?' But the questions were rhetorical, there was no need for Antony to make even a guarded reply.

Instead he remarked, 'It would interest me to know, Fran, what Veronica had to say about the Keats family. I had to be very careful in talking to them to disguise the real motive for my questions, and it occurred to me that Veronica knew them for three years or so, and most probably had something to say about each one of them from time to time.'

'We didn't see each other very often, you know, not until Mr Lund advised her to move out of the house in Wimbledon and leave them in possession and she came to stay with me. I knew most of them by name, of course. She always said the old gentleman was why she stayed so long, she'd have liked something a little more difficult to cope with, something that tested her nursing skill. But he was always very nice to her, and . . . well, I think she enjoyed their rather luxurious way of life.'

'I'm not surprised. What about the other members of the

family?'

'I don't think she liked any of them very much. That shouldn't prejudice you, Mr Maitland, Veronica didn't make many friends. She said Mrs Keats—Mrs Maurice Keats—was dreadfully lazy and the cook, I think she called her Daisy, didn't know her place. The housekeeper was pleasant enough, but only because she was fond of the old man and wanted him to have the best nursing care.'

'And the other two men in the house, Maurice and Stephen Keats?'

'She saw Maurice at breakfast and dinner-time most days, and she said he was always perfectly polite but there were so many business things he wanted to talk over with his father that she found it rather boring. Stephen was away a lot, and he and his girl-friend, Sally, would sometimes ask her to accompany them to the cinema or to the local pub. She said it was all rather a bore, but she didn't like to refuse though she'd have liked to because she thought that Sally's attitude was a little condescending.'

'In three years she must have met the other members of the family . . . the ones who didn't live in the Wimbledon house.'

'Oh yes, she said the other Mrs Keats—Mrs Ralph Keats—was there nearly every weekend. The way Veronica put it was that she used to make up to the old man. Her son, Julian, lived with her, lives with her I should say, and Veronica didn't seem to dislike him particularly, though she said he was callow. He and his girl-friend, Jean, used to take her out sometimes too or sometimes they'd all go out together. It would just be for a couple of hours after dinner, before she had to get old Mr Keats to bed.'

'That covers the field, I think.' Maitland glanced at Johnny Lund for confirmation. 'Let's return to the night you were injured. Have you been able to remember any more about it?'

'Yes, I have, thank goodness. I know the doctor said it was quite natural, but even a few minutes out of your life that you

162

can't remember gives you an awfully uneasy feeling.'

'Tell us then.'

'The door was locked as usual when I got home, there was nothing at all to indicate that anyone had got in. That does puzzle me, Mr Maitland, because I'm quite sure there were only two keys. The police had Veronica's, and I still have mine.'

'Just a moment. Did Veronica have a key before she came to stay with you after her employer's death?'

'Yes, because I thought she might like to come here sometimes on her day off, and if she hadn't bothered to telephone – which it's quite likely she wouldn't have done – she could get in anyway even if I was out, and wait until I came back.'

'I see. Go on with your recollections of that night.'

'The door to the sitting-room was closed too, but I don't remember that it struck me as odd at the time. Only later, thinking it over, I realised that I always leave that door open so as to spread the warmth about a little. When they put in central heating in the house they forgot all about the stairway, and though it doesn't terribly matter at the end of the winter I'd still be leaving that door open out of habit.'

'So it gave you no warning?'

'No, it didn't. The first thing that was odd was when I opened the door and there was the bureau with the flap wrenched off and thrown to one side and everything in wild disorder. And before I'd even time to be frightened there was a movement behind me, I think the man must have been hiding behind the door when I opened it. And I remember being suddenly terrified and starting to turn round, but that's really all. I suppose there was a moment of pain when he hit me, but I didn't know anything else until after Mr Lund got to the flat and had called the doctor for me.'

'This bureau, you said it belonged to your sister?'

'It was left to her by a great-aunt, the one who left me the

163

whatnot – I think that's the correct description – that stands in the corner. It's rather ugly really but I've kept it because she meant it kindly. Or course, Veronica had nowhere to put the bureau when she was in training, and that's how it came to be there. Then she took up private nursing, so it still stayed.'

'It must be quite an old piece, then. Is it valuable?'

'I don't know, I've never thought about it.'

'And you're sure there was nothing in it of Veronica's?'

'No, I've been using it for years. If she had any letter writing to do or bills to pay I expect she did it in her own room at the Wimbledon house. After all, Mr Keats didn't need too much attention, and there must have been lots of time to fill.'

'You still haven't missed anything from there?'

'Not a thing. I'm afraid I'm rather untidy and couldn't really be sure, but why should anybody want my private correspondence, or an unpaid bill, or something like that?'

'No, I see your point. It might just have been a casual marauder,' he said, half to Johnny and half to their client. 'When you disturbed him he probably didn't have the nerve to go through the rest of the place.'

'Do you really believe that, Mr Maitland?'

'Well, no, as a matter of fact I don't,' he admitted. 'I think that all the things that happened were connected, because why should anyone have chosen that particular time to burgle you? It's a pity there were no signs of forcible entry, but it's too late to worry about that now. One more question and then we're done. What did Veronica do on her days off, as opposed to those evening outings you've talked about?'

'I haven't the faintest idea. I suppose she'd come to see me about three or four times a year but not, of course until evening. I told you I'd given her a key, and it's possible she may have used it in my absence, but that couldn't have been very often or I'd have noticed. And nearly always when she came I'd be working upstairs but I always heard her.'

'No friends you know of whom she'd be likely to visit?'

'Not that I know of. But you see, Mr Maitland . . . I know she could be secretive, but we weren't so close that we told each other everything. If you were asking her about me she'd be just as vague. Only of course you can't do that now,' she added rather sadly.

The hearing itself didn't take long either, though its commencement was unduly delayed in Maitland's opinion by the hearing of a case so minor as to be able to be dealt with summarily. The plea of Not Guilty was entered, the Crown produced the smallest amount of evidence that it thought it could get away with, the facts that had in the first place suggested murder, the fact that there were no fingerprints in the flat except those of the deceased and her sister, the fact that nobody could be found who had seen a visitor arrive during the time Miss Frances Procter alleged that she was absent, and the fact that a motive existed in that, since Veronica Procter died intestate, Frances Procter was her sole heir and stood to inherit a considerable sum under the will of Samuel Keats. Veronica Procter's late employer. At that point Maitland started to get to his feet, but he caught the eye of the rather junior counsel who was handling the case for the prosecution at that stage and who added in a hurry, 'I must qualify that by saying that circumstances had arisen which made it very unlikely that Veronica Procter would so inherit, but it is the Crown's contention that the accused is not sufficiently conversant with the law to have realised that at the time.' But then he added perhaps the most damning thing of all. 'In any case, the sisters are known to have been on bad terms, and were heard quarrelling on more than one occasion by their neighbour who occupies the ground floor flat in the same house.'

Apart from that one, almost involuntary, movement Maitland held his fire. The necessary witnesses were called, with all the delay that entailed, and Frances Procter was duly committed for trial and promptly whisked out of court. 'But at least,'

165

said Johnny, as they went out into the street together, 'as her solicitor I can see her whenever I want.'

'You know, Johnny, I don't think that might be such a good idea.'

'Why ever not? I know what Briggs said about giving up the case but –'

'We might have to, for Fran Procter's sake as well as our own. And don't remind me, as she did, of what I said in a temper yesterday, because it's very unlikely I'll be able to deliver.'

'All right I won't, but I still think –'

'Thoughts can be dangerous,' Antony assured him smiling. 'If evidence could be brought that you had been to see your client more than was reasonable a suggestion of bias would follow and very likely be believed.'

'But it isn't a strong case, is it? Even with the evidence of the chap who heard them quarrelling. After all, Fran told us that was about the will. She didn't want Veronica to take the money.'

'On the evidence she should be acquitted, if she makes a good showing in the witness box, and if the jury pay the slightest heed to the judge's direction to them. But as we can't count on either of those things I'd better get busy again this afternoon.'

'Can't I help?'

'No, Johnny, you can't, and for the same reason that I don't want you visiting Fran Procter too much. Roger has never seen her and therefore his evidence, if anything useful turns up, will be regarded as unprejudiced. He's barely acquainted with Maurice and Isabel Keats, and knows Julian sufficiently well to say Good Morning to him when they meet, but that might make anything he said that tended to clear Fran all the more impressive.'

'Yes, I see what you mean. Don't worry, Antony, I'll do as you say. And meanwhile –'

'Meanwhile you'll come and have lunch with me,' said Antony, looking around for a taxi. 'You'll be doing me a good turn,' he added, when Johnny seemed about to demur. 'Uncle Nick'll probably be at Astroff's, and he hasn't had a chance yet of telling me, with whatever embellishments he can think of, that what happened yesterday is somehow or other my fault.'

Johnny made no further objection but his silence during the meal was not due, Maitland thought, to the awe in which he still held Sir Nicholas, as under other circumstances it might have been. He was brooding on Fran Procter's predicament, and Antony only hoped that his words on the subject had gone home, and that Johnny wouldn't decide to try a little detection himself.

However, his presence did have the desired effect of bottling up Sir Nicholas's irritation for the time being at least. Meg and Roger he had come to regard as members of the family, which could be an advantage, though on the other hand it meant that he was quite willing to speak his mind in front of them, either about their own imperfections or, more frequently, about his nephew's. But Johnny was younger and had not yet achieved that status, a fact for which Antony would have told him he should be truly thankful.

II

A telephone call had been made, and true to his promise Roger had arranged to encounter Antony as casually as possible at the offices of Keats & Company. He was already outside the building where their offices were housed when Antony's taxi drew up, and disappeared through the glass doors immediately without giving any sign of recognition. By the time Maitland – a little confused by the modernity of the building because Roger's office, which he had often visited, was just about as unpretentious as his own room in chambers – got up to the right floor Roger was already talking to the receptionist. Antony, eyeing his performance with a critical eye, thought that his startled surprise at seeing his friend was a little overdone, but in the absence of either of the people who interested him this didn't worry him unduly. Having greeted his friend, giving no sign at all that they had met the previous evening, he turned and strolled across to the desk to say to the girl there, 'I was hoping to see Mr Keats.'

'Mr Maurice or Mr Julian?' she asked.

'I think perhaps it would be better if I saw Mr Maurice Keats first.'

'I'm afraid you'll have to wait, this gentleman also has business with Mr Maurice.'

'Then as he got here first –' Antony began, but the receptionist had already picked up what was presumably the internal phone.

'Mr Roger Farrell is here to see you, Mr Maurice,' she said. 'And another gentleman,' she looked inquiringly at Antony who supplied his name, 'another gentleman named Maitland arrived just after he did.'

A moment later she put down the receiver and turned on them a puzzled look. 'He didn't say anything, only that he'd come right out,' she reported. And true enough, hard on the heels of this statement Maurice Keats bustled down the corridor to where Antony and Roger were conversing quietly together. 'Well, well!' he said. 'To what do I owe the honour? My dear wife told me that you two were friends, but I imagine Mr Farrell, you didn't come here for the same kindly reason.' It was impossible to tell whether some intonation of sarcasm lay behind the words.

'Hardly,' said Roger, smiling at him, and carefully taking what he said at face value. 'As a matter of fact we came

168

separately.' Which was true enough. 'There's a small matter I'd like your advice about, you've something of a reputation as an expert on tobacco futures. The thing is –'

'That shouldn't take us very long. If you don't mind I'll find out what Mr Maitland wants first. Come along to my office both of you, I know from what my wife told me that this sad matter is to some degree familiar to you,' he added to Roger as they went.

'My errand won't take long either,' said Antony. Roger moved across the room and began examining the books that lined one wall. 'I think between you, you and Mrs Keats filled me in very well as to the circumstances surrounding your father's death. And your son and his fiancée were quite ready to help too, but unfortunately it seems that Veronica Procter was extraordinarily secretive about her own affairs.'

'That's a pity. I had hoped –'

'Did you know that Frances Procter has been arrested?' Antony asked, interrupting him.

'I read it in the paper this morning. In a way I'm sorry for the girl, because she certainly acted on a mistaken belief. Long before that, very shortly after the cause of my father's death was established, Bernard Stanley told me we'd have no difficulty now in getting the new will set aside.'

'I won't argue with you about Veronica,' said Antony, feeling a little guilty about the deception he was practising on Johnny, 'but I still believe in Fran's innocence.'

'You're her lawyer,' said Maurice, as though that explained everything.

'Yes, but if I knew she was guilty – knew as opposed to wondering – there'd be nothing for it but to have her plead that way. And even if I wondered . . . in that case it would be up to her solicitor. I'd study my brief and make out the best case I could and that would be that.'

'Are you so sure of her?' Roger turned his head as Maurice spoke, so that Antony thought immediately that that was a

169

question that had occurred to him too.

'As sure as one can be of anything in this uncertain world,' he said. 'So that's why, Mr Keats, I'd like to see your nephew Julian. There's just a chance she might have confided in him, or in that girl of his –'

'Jean Ingelow,' Maurice supplied.

'Yes, exactly. But I didn't feel I should ask to see Julian before I spoke to you again.'

'We'll have him in.' He spoke into the telephone for a moment. 'I don't suppose he's doing anything that can't wait.'

'Shall I have to explain myself to him?' Maitland asked.

'Not a bit of it. Didn't you find my family at home well-briefed?'

'Yes, I did, and I was very grateful for it.'

'Well, I see Julian every day of course, and I told him to put the matter up to his mother. I very much doubt that Blythe can help you, though she visited quite a lot, but Veronica wouldn't know her as well as she did those of us who lived in the house.'

'Sometimes it's easier to confide in a comparative stranger,' said Antony. 'I'm in a state of mind,' he added, 'to leave no stone unturned or avenue unexplored.'

'I hope this new client of yours is all you think her,' said Maurice. 'After all, in view of what Veronica did –' But at that point, perhaps fortunately, he was interrupted by a tap on the door and a very tall, very thin, fair-haired young man came in, so that the phrase *I was a pale young curate then* leaped immediately into Antony's mind and almost as quickly the first line of the lyric added itself to his mental filing system, *Time was when love and I were well acquainted.* Sometimes these seemingly ineffectual young men were perfectly capable of reaping havoc in the breast of every woman they came into contact with.

While these inconclusive ideas were flashing through his mind Maurice had been effecting introductions. 'As it happens

170

Mr Farrell came to see me on another matter,' he explained, 'but as I know he's in Mr Maitland's confidence it seemed kinder to bring him in here than leave him in the waiting-room.'

'Much kinder,' said Julian. He had an unexpectedly deep voice, rather pleasant to listen to. 'That waiting-room may be the last word in up-to-date furniture, but most of it is damned uncomfortable.'

'Never mind that, you don't have to sit there.'

'No, but some of my clients do, and by the time they get to my room they're decidedly ill-tempered.'

'Then you should schedule your appointments more carefully,' Maurice pointed out. 'Now I don't think Mr Maitland will want to keep you very long. He's anxious to find out if you know anything about Veronica Procter's friends.'

'I suppose you could apply that description to Stephen and Sally and Jean and me. Sally thought she was lonely, and that made Jean go all soft-hearted too. The result was we were burdened with her far more than I liked. She wasn't my type.'

'Well,' it seemed to Maitland time to take over the questioning, 'did she ever say anything to indicate whose type she was.'

'If you mean do I know anything about her other friends, no I don't. I don't think Veronica was given to confidential conversations, and if she had been and I'd wanted to listen we'd have had very little opportunity. It's all very well being kind to people, but a threesome is a very uncomfortable sort of arrangement, and a fivesome – if there is such a word – is even worse.'

'I've been wondering what she did on her days off. These jaunts of yours were extras, weren't they?'

'To tell you the truth Jean and I have discussed that several times. Once or twice she said she'd been to see her sister, but mostly she said nothing at all about it. She was a stunner to look at, you know, and I'm afraid Jean and I indulged in some

171

rather – er – erotic speculations,' he went on with a sidelong glance at his uncle to see how he was taking it. 'But as for knowing anything, I'm sure she's as much in the dark as I am.'

'That's a pity, but I think I'd like to see her all the same. I've heard it stated that girls like to keep an aura of mystery around them in order to attract the man of their choice. Jean may not tell you everything she knows.'

'There's no difficulty about seeing her, but I think you'll find I'm right. I say, though, I'd like to meet this twin sister of Veronica's.'

'You can't,' said Maurice rather impatiently. 'She's under arrest.'

'I know that, but it doesn't stop me wishing, does it? Is she really as like Veronica as they say?'

'As who say?'

'I saw it in the newspaper. You know how careful they have to be, but I suppose that was one thing they could write safely and know they wouldn't be sued for libel.'

'Yes, I suppose so. Anyway you can take it from me as far as looks go there's not a penny to choose between them. But as to character . . . well I think their choice of occupations will explain that as well as I can. Fran is a would-be artist, Veronica was a nurse. Everyone says she was a good one,' he added thoughtfully, 'but I suppose it depends what you mean by good.'

'You mean poisoning grandfather shouldn't have been on the agenda,' said Julian. 'I quite agree with you about that. Anyway go and see Jean, I wouldn't be surprised if she wasn't quite thrilled about it.'

'Very well then, I'll go along to your mother's place straight away, and I'm grateful for your blessing on my activities.' He made his farewells and went away presently leaving Roger and Maurice presumably discussing tobacco futures, whatever they might be.

By previous arrangement, Maitland waited outside the

building until Roger joined him not more than a quarter of an hour later. They walked back together to the place where Roger had managed to insert his car. 'This isn't going to work,' he said bluntly. 'Blythe is bound to tell the other Keatses that we visited her together.'

'Well, as she's the last one on the list along with this Ingelow girl that doesn't worry me very much. Rather different for you though, I hadn't thought of that. Would you mind very much if Maurice Keats cut you dead on the floor of the Stock Exchange?'

'Not particularly,' said Roger. They walked in silence for a few moments, and then he went on almost accusingly, 'You've got some sort of an idea in your mind, haven't you?'

'In a way. I'm sorry, Roger, but it's too nebulous to talk about.'

'Something hit you when Julian Keats came into the office,' said Roger positively.

'Was it as obvious as all that? As a matter of fact what came into my mind was a quotation from W. S. Gilbert. You couldn't have a much more innocent thought than that.'

'Have it your own way.' They'd reached the car now and he walked round to slip into the driver's seat. 'Give me that address again,' he said. 'And what's the betting we shall have to park at least a mile away?'

III

Though Blythe Keats's establishment was outwardly no different from any other office (but who knew what went on behind all the closed doors they passed on their way to her room) Maitland walked into her presence, after thanking their escort, rather as if he were going into a lion's den. He then halted abruptly in the doorway so that Roger had his work cut out not to bump into him, and looked all around him cautiously. 'Mrs Keats,' he said, and the different air that he could assume at will was very marked. 'It's good of you to see me.'

'I understand from my brother-in-law that it's not too great an ordeal.' She was a big woman, but there was something in her manner – a trace of skittishness perhaps – that repelled him. 'But he didn't mention that you'd have a companion, Mr Maitland.'

Antony stopped looking around him ("gawking," said Roger unkindly afterwards) and fixed his eyes on her. 'Well you see,' he said earnestly, 'this isn't at all what I imagined.'

'What did you expect?' She sounded amused now.

'Oh, girls floating around in long gowns, a lot of fashionable women sitting about on small gilt chairs. That kind of thing. So I asked my friend Roger Farrell to come with me – this is Mr Farrell – because he's the sort of man who doesn't mind going with his wife to buy a nightgown, which is something I've always managed to avoid.'

'Obviously a heroic character,' Blythe Keats commented dryly. 'How do you do, Mr Farrell?'

'An associate of mine,' said Antony, which was true enough though not quite in the way he meant her to understand it. 'Did your brother-in-law explain to you exactly what I want?' he asked.

'You'd better both sit down,' she said and seated herself again behind the desk. 'I assure you the chairs aren't likely to collapse,' she added.

'They aren't at all the kind of thing I was thinking of,' said Maitland hastily. 'And a good deal more comfortable than anything I've got in my office,' he added a moment later. 'But you were going to tell me – '

'What Maurice told me. He said that Veronica Procter's sister wasn't at all convinced that she had killed Samuel, and that you felt it would be better for her to take a more realistic

174

view of the situation. But now Veronica is dead and this girl herself has been arrested –'

'She's a nice girl, Mrs Keats, I don't think she harmed anyone. I want to find who killed Veronica, but my original objective still stands, of course.'

'I don't really see how I can help you.'

'But you visited the house at Wimbledon often?'

'Yes I did, I was very fond of Samuel and I went to see him whenever I could. Most weekends, in fact, though sometimes I'd go there to dinner during the week as well.'

'What was your impression of Veronica Procter?'

'A clever girl. Clever enough to keep anyone from knowing what she was really thinking. I have to say, though, that she seemed to look after my father-in-law extremely well. It was a terrible shock when he died, but a greater shock than that when we knew what had really happened.'

'Did you visit him during his last illness, Mrs Keats?'

'Yes, but Veronica wouldn't let me stay more than a minute or two. He was obviously very weak, and she came into the corridor with me when I left and told me that the continual sickness had worn him out. But even then I never thought he was dying.'

'And when you heard about the will?'

'Well, I expect you can imagine that I was absolutely horrified. It wasn't the money,' (and that's a lie if ever I heard one), 'but the unfairness of it. And then I began to think back, and I could see that there had been ways in which she tried to influence him. Nothing conclusive, nothing that could have been used when the case came on, but I felt I'd been rather silly not to see what was happening. And then, of course, as Maurice said, his dying so soon after he'd made a new will was just too much.'

'But then somebody killed Veronica,' said Antony. 'That's what really concerns me now, and I thought perhaps she might have talked to you more openly than she seems to have done

175

to anyone else. About her friends,' he added encouragingly.

'I don't think I want to get mixed up in that,' said Mrs Keats recoiling a little.

'Surely, an innocent girl –'

'I've only your word for that and I don't see how you can know. The police have their reasons, I'm sure of that, and anyway I couldn't possibly give evidence in court.'

To lie or not to lie? 'If there's anything you can tell me,' said Antony, 'it might come to that. But it's nothing to worry about, being a witness. No worse in fact than my visiting you this afternoon, when I had to bring Roger along with me for protection.'

He smiled at her, but her answering smile was a very wavering one. 'I should have to give my name, shouldn't I?' she said.

'Well yes, of course,' said Maitland puzzled.

'My real name?' she insisted.

'Yes, I'm afraid so, but is that so very terrible? You use it in your business, don't you?'

'Don't be silly,' she snapped at him suddenly. 'Nobody in this world could possibly be called Blythe.' She paused and it was Roger who broke the silence.

'What name did your parents give you?' he asked.

She closed her eyes. Perhaps she was trying to pretend she was making her admission to an empty room. 'Gay,' she whispered. 'But I changed it years ago, when the word began to mean something quite different. I don't think anyone remembers now, and Ralph's family never knew about it.'

'If you changed it by deed poll –'

'I didn't. Someone told me you have a perfect right to call yourself anything you like, and that would just mean publicity. I couldn't possibly get up in court and tell everyone –'

'Nobody would think twice about it, Mrs Keats,' said Roger in a rallying tone.

'Oh yes, they would!'

'Well, Mr Maitland is very good at seeing ways round difficulties. If you've anything to tell him I'm sure he can find some way of introducing it into evidence without involving you.'

'Do you really think so?' She looked at him hopefully.

'I'm quite sure of it.'

'What did you want to know?' She was addressing herself to Roger now, and speaking far more simply than she had originally done.

'Whether Veronica ever spoke to you about her friends. You see it's very unlikely that a complete stranger killed her.'

'No, she didn't.'

'Or about where she went on her days off?'

'I'm afraid I can't tell you that either. Except,' she added, 'that one day when she'd been at Wimbledon about a year she came to see me to ask my advice about a very special dress she wanted. It was quite a pleasure to talk to her about style and colour, she was a real beauty you know.'

Maitland interposed there. 'Did she agree with your ideas?' he asked.

'As far as I know. When we were talking it certainly seemed that she did. But if she had the dress made up I never saw it. Of course she wouldn't wear it about the house, she had her uniform. But I did think after I'd taken so much time over it that she might have shown me the finished product.'

'Can you remember the date when this happened?'

'Just about this time of year, and it must have been two years ago because I'm sure it wasn't last year and three years ago I hardly knew her. But that can't have anything to do with her being killed.'

'No, of course not. I talked to your son earlier this afternoon, Mrs Keats, but he knew nothing of Veronica's friends either though he and Miss Ingelow had taken her out sometimes out of kindness. We wondered if perhaps—'

'You mean that Jean might be able to tell you something. I

don't think so, Mr Maitland, because I'm sure she'd have told me. She's a very nice girl and I wish she didn't have these silly ideas about marriage being unfashionable. I'm so glad that Sally brought Stephen to the point of proposing at last, and when she sees how beautiful a wedding can be perhaps Jean will change her mind.'

'Perhaps she will. But the thing is now, Mrs Keats, may I have a word with her?'

'Yes, of course you can, though I told you I'm sure she won't be able to help.' If she noticed a difference in his manner now she gave no sign. 'Anything she knew she'd have confided to me, at least I think she would. But you say you've talked to Julian already and certainly she'd have told him.'

But there was nothing to be got out of Jean Ingelow when she was produced a few minutes later, a slim, brown girl with a snub nose and a twinkle in her eye. All Antony's questions drew negative replies, and the only thing she contributed to the store of their knowledge was that she'd been terrified when Sally first suggested that they might take Veronica out sometimes. 'Which might be all right for her, she's quite good-looking herself, but I can't hold a candle to Veronica. Besides Sally wasn't even engaged to Stephen then. But it was all right, Julian never looked twice at her. I mean he did, of course, but not in that way.'

Maitland couldn't help smiling at her. 'I expect Julian knows when he's well off,' he said, and repeated as much to Roger when they were out in the street again. 'It's a good thing you made such a hit with dear Blythe,' he added. 'Who'd have thought she'd be so mealy-mouthed about admitting that her name was really Gay.'

'That's all very well but we didn't really learn anything, and you must have left her thinking you a perfect fool,' said Roger despondently. 'If you ask me, Antony, you've come up against a brick wall. There's nowhere to go from here.'

'Home,' Maitland suggested. 'Is Meg's throat better yet?'

178

'No, she's taking the rest of the week off.'

'Then fetch her around to our place.'

'Jenny—'

'I'll give you a ring if there isn't enough dinner to go round,' Antony promised. 'But you know Jenny, she always provides as if for an army.'

'You have got something in mind,' said Roger accusingly.

'Something . . . or nothing. You'll hear all about it if it works out when I've had a chance to think about it. Or – a better idea than parting at this point – take me home first and we'll use the dreaded house phone to ask Jenny about dinner. Then you can go and fetch Meg.'

They needn't have worried. 'Tell Roger Meg's throat is a lot better today,' Jenny informed them cheerfully. 'We arranged between us hours ago that they should both come to dinner again tonight.'

IV

But when Roger and Meg arrived back at Kempenfeldt Square they found Jenny alone. 'Antony stayed only long enough to make a telephone call,' she said, 'I think it was to Inspector Sykes. Then he went out again in rather a hurry, and said not to wait dinner for him. I'll get you a drink and then you can tell us, Roger, if you know what it's all about?'

'I know something struck him during the talks we had this afternoon,' said Roger slowly. 'I think it was something to do with Julian Keats, but if I tell you what was said you may be able to make a guess at what it was. Antony wouldn't tell me, he said his ideas were too vague.'

'I'd love to hear, but Uncle Nick and Vera will be here in a moment. If you wait till they come it will only need going over once.'

179

'It isn't Tuesday,' said Meg. Her voice was much better today, though probably she couldn't have filled the theatre with it, and she knew the habits of the entire household at Kempenfeldt Square as well as they did themselves.

'No, but I know they're worried about this business with Superintendent Briggs,' said Jenny. 'Well, so am I, of course, but at least it doesn't seem as if anyone will have a chance to shoot Antony, or hit him over the head, or anything violent like that while he's with Inspector Sykes. And you've been with him most of the day, Roger, so – '

'That kind of thing isn't so easy to get away with,' Roger interrupted her seriously. 'Besides, whoever killed Veronica must feel he's got away with it now that Fran Procter has been arrested. To attack Antony would be a dead giveaway.'

'Yes, of course, I know that.' If both of them were thinking that the injury Fran Procter had sustained had had no such effect Jenny had no time to express her doubts because Sir Nicholas and Vera arrived at that moment.

Roger's account of the afternoon's events didn't take very long and when he had finished Sir Nicholas was nodding, as though in agreement with some unstated fact. But he declined to be drawn on the subject, saying only, 'I won't deny Antony the pleasure of telling us the whole story.' Which, as he knew perfectly well his nephew's dislike for explanations, made Jenny momentarily indignant.

But Vera wrenched the subject violently away from Fran Procter and her affairs, Meg backed her up valiantly – she seemed to be enjoying making up for lost time now that her throat was less painful – and soon they were discussing the morning's headlines, which Meg said, probably inaccurately, were all she ever bothered to read: these had mainly concerned the first release by the White House of edited transcripts of the Watergate tapes, which Sir Nicholas insisted had no evidential value whatever and were probably downright misleading; the Guillaume spy affair in Germany was also touched

180

on, and its probable consequences for the Chancellor, but it cannot be said that any of them were really paying sufficient attention to these earth-shaking events. By the time dinner was ready Antony had still not returned, but he came in just as they had finished the meal, meeting Roger, who was carrying a laden tray, in the hall. Jenny, having heard the door give its characteristic squeak, appeared promptly from the kitchen.

'You must be starving Antony. Would you like to eat straight away?'

'I don't think so love.' He sounded both tired and troubled. 'I'm not really hungry but I could do with a drink. Do you think that Uncle Nick would assume I'm becoming an alcoholic if I have a scotch? That seems to be what's called for.'

By this time Roger had put down the tray on the kitchen table and joined them again. Jenny thought sadly for a moment of the food that was keeping warm in the oven, and would be far too dry to eat by the time her husband was ready for it, and said decisively, 'Roger will pour you one. And I'll make you a sandwich in case you feel like eating it.'

So Antony and Roger went into the living-room together, and Antony greeted his uncle and aunt with the slight formality which he still observed towards Vera, and without any apparent surprise at finding them there; inquired politely about Meg's cold, and showed due gratification when she answered him in nearly-normal tones. He then sank into the chair that Roger had been occupying, received the scotch with a word of thanks, drank it as though he were thirsty and handed the glass back for a refill. Catching his uncle's eye he smiled faintly. 'Well, Uncle Nick?' he said.

'Something to tell us,' said Vera. 'But don't talk until you're ready.'

'As well now as later, better perhaps. I've been talking non-stop to Sykes and Mayhew, and it's all very clear in my mind.'

'Where have you been?' asked Sir Nicholas.

'To Fran Procter's flat. I caught Sykes just before he left the Yard, and asked him to bring Mayhew along as a witness since his friendship with me is known.'

'Roger has already given us an account of your afternoon's activities,' his uncle told him, 'so you can confine yourself to the conclusions you've drawn.'

'If you heard all that you've probably got an inkling yourself of what I'm going to tell you.'

'A vague sort of idea,' said Sir Nicholas. 'The question is, have you succeeded in convincing Sykes and Mayhew?'

'On the contrary, Uncle Nick,' said Meg, 'the immediate question is what he was trying to convince them about. You may think you know, but I haven't the faintest idea, and I admit I'm very curious.'

'Very well, my dear, we'll take everything in order,' said Sir Nicholas amiably. 'Start at the beginning, Antony.'

Jenny had returned by this time, and both a sandwich and the second glass of scotch remained neglected on the table at Antony's side. 'You know all about the beginning,' he protested.

'We know that you decided that Frances Procter was innocent, on what appeared to have been very insufficient grounds,' said Sir Nicholas. 'Now from what Roger tells us you have obtained a clue which was at least convincing enough to bring Chief Inspector Sykes and Inspector Mayhew out to meet you at the end of their working day. What we want to know is what you told them, why the meeting took place at Miss Procter's flat, and whether any action will result from it?'

'I think you've guessed the answer to the first of those questions, Uncle Nick.'

'I'm not given to jumping to conclusions.'

'You two may know what you're talking about,' said Meg, 'but I don't for one. Roger thought it was something to do with Julian Keats.'

'Yes, that's when the first inkling of the truth came to me, when he walked into the room, though I should have thought of it earlier. If Fran was innocent there were a number of things to be explained. First it seemed obvious that the two murders must be connected, and equally that Veronica had killed old Mr Keats. This left a – a sort of vacuum where the motive for poisoning her was concerned except for Johnny's idea that it might have been done out of revenge. But that seemed so unlikely as to be not worth considering, in view of the fact that it was now almost certain that the new will would be overset. There was also the question of how the person who ransacked the bureau and then hit Fran over the head had obtained access to the flat without leaving any signs of forcible entry.'

'And now you've succeeded in explaining all these things, at least to your own satisfaction?' said Sir Nicholas.

'Yes, and Roger's quite right, it was seeing Julian that made me realise how everything could be explained quite simply. If Samuel Keats's death had been the result of a conspiracy between Veronica and a member of the family – '

'But why should seeing this man Julian make you think that?' asked Meg. 'Does he look like a murderer?'

'Not a bit of it.'

'Well then!'

'It was because the first thing that came into my mind when I saw him was the phrase, *I was a pale young curate then*. And I began to think how some of those very quiet, not particularly distinguished men are enormously attractive to women. Like the song from which those words come.'

'Direction of thoughts quite obvious,' said Vera, and to no-one's surprise began to sing quietly. She had a good voice, and with a slight change of key could manage Dr Daly's ballad quite well. *I had no care – no jealous doubts hung o'er me – for I was loved beyond all other men. Fled gilded dukes and belted earls before me – ah me, I was a pale young curate then!*

'That's exactly it,' said Antony, with the first enthusiasm he

183

had shown that evening. 'As I said, if Veronica was in cahoots with some member of the family –'

'If ever you wish to go to America again,' said Sir Nicholas faintly, 'I warn you I shall flatly forbid the expedition.' He then closed his eyes and appeared to swoon.

'Well, you must admit it would explain things,' said Antony stubbornly, 'as I think you realise perfectly well, Uncle Nick. I suppose it might be argued that Sally Hargreaves and Jean Ingelow were possibles, but neither of them could be certain of profiting from what was done. The left the four legatees under the original will, and it was hardly likely that Maurice Keats or his sister-in-law, who stood to gain a great deal in their own right, would have needed an accomplice if murder was in either of their minds. The two grandsons, however, might have felt it desirable to get a much larger legacy through Veronica, which – if the old man's death had never been discovered to be murder – would quite likely have been possible. But the only way they could have been sure of her was by marriage. I wonder if you thought it worth mentioning, Roger, that Veronica had consulted Blythe Keats about a dress for a very special occasion. That was two years ago and it might well have been for her wedding.'

'Guesswork again,' said Sir Nicholas, who appeared to have recovered while his nephew was speaking, but the remark was too familiar to call for any reply, and Antony went on unheeding.

'As I was saying, all this flashed through my mind when the sight of Julian Keats first put the thought of love and marriage into my head. Why shouldn't Veronica have fallen in love with one of the grandsons and married him? If she had, I think the idea of killing the old man must have been already in his mind, at least otherwise it's odd that the marriage was kept secret. But, of course, nothing could be done immediately, she had to consolidate her position with Samuel Keats first, and then start her careful campaign towards getting him to make her his heir.

184

And what I think is – and I'll admit, Uncle Nick, before you point it out, that I've no proof of it – that she started giving him something to upset him three months or a little more before his death, and then got it fixed in his mind in some way that the family were trying to poison him. That would explain, too, why he made her his heir. She must have seemed to him like his last refuge.'

'That wasn't what he told Bernard Stanley.'

'No, but I can imagine that when it came to the point he couldn't bring himself to make so terrible an accusation. After all, it was his nearest and dearest he'd be talking about. But I'm sure Bernard would argue about the change, and he had to find some explanation to give him. Veronica was a nurse, and would know how to get her effects perfectly well, and once the will was made there was nothing to stop her working up gradually to his death.'

'Do you think all this was done by Julian Keats?'

'Did I imply that? I didn't mean to. I rather favoured Stephen myself when I thought about it. He certainly knew Fran's address, and that she spent most evenings upstairs in her studio, though of course it's quite possible that Veronica had told him those things quite innocently. But I think the real reason for my conviction that he was the one involved was that the death of the old man was so carefully accomplished while he was out of the country. And you can add to that the fact that he had taken Sally Hargreaves out regularly when he was at home, so that everyone thought they'd make a match of it, but carefully didn't become engaged to her until after Veronica was dead. By the way, if Veronica were married to one of the grandsons that would explain how he got admission to Fran's flat. Obviously Veronica had had a key cut from her own, and given it to him when she went to stay there.'

'Then why was Veronica Procter killed?'

'I think Stephen lost his nerve when the manner of his grandfather's death was discovered. It was quite obvious then

185

that the new will wouldn't be granted probate, and if Veronica was arrested there was a chance that she'd talk. It must have seemed best to him to cut his losses and get rid of her too. If they'd discussed the method of killing the old man, he'd have known quite well where to find the weed-killer and make the solution to give to his wife.'

'Very well then, why was Frances Procter attacked?'

'Because she disturbed Stephen while he was searching the bureau. It belonged to Veronica remember, and it occurred to me that she might well have told him there was some secret compartment in it. If you'd met her you'd realise she was unlikely to have told that to her sister.'

'I still don't see why, darling,' said Meg. 'After all, Veronica was unlikely to have kept a diary, or written down exactly what they were doing. So what did he expect to find there?'

'I'm on safer ground here, as even you'll admit, Uncle Nick. I don't know whether Veronica had told him what she'd done, in which case you'd have expected him to look for the hiding-place the night she died, though perhaps the timing wasn't right. Even if he didn't mind about her dying, he'd have hardly wanted to hang around and watch. Anyway, it's probably more likely that it came to him later that it would have been the ideal place for her to put their marriage certificate, and that's just where Sykes found it when we went to the flat tonight.'

'So Veronica told him of the secret compartment, but not how to open it?'

'That must have been the case, it was only a narrow gap behind the drawers between the pigeon-holes. And the gadget you had to press wasn't at all obvious to the eye, that's partly why I was so late, it took us some time to find it. And I should tell you that we also found something else at the same time, or rather a few minutes later when we went up to the studio and unpacked Veronica's trunks that were standing there. Of course, the police had looked at them before, but there was no reason why what they found should mean anything to them. Only I thought perhaps that very special dress might have been worn just once and then put away, and there it was, a sort of creamy white creation –'

'How do you know its significance?'

'I'll bet I'm right, and I'll bet Mrs Blythe Keats will confirm what she remembers of the details of her conversation with Veronica about it. But the clinching thing was that in one pocket, wrapped carefully in tissue paper, was a brand new wedding ring. I think that at least Stephen Keats is going to have some explaining to do . . . don't you think?'

'Sounds pretty conclusive,' said Vera. 'Don't you think so, Nicholas?'

'It's certainly enough to get Frances Procter acquitted,' agreed Sir Nicholas, 'enough to get the Crown to refrain from presenting any evidence against her even if it's decided not to charge this young man. Was Chief Inspector Sykes convinced, do you think?'

'Yes. I think he was, and Mayhew too.'

His uncle smiled suddenly. 'And as he always says, once you know where to look there's evidence to be found,' he remarked.

'And even Briggs,' said Antony, 'won't be able to think any longer that I had any hand in hitting Fran over the head. At least, I shouldn't think so,' he added with a shade of doubt in his voice.

Sir Nicholas exchanged a glance with his wife. 'We must hope you're right about that,' he said. And might have been about to add something if Meg had not forestalled him.

'What about Johnny?' she demanded.

'There's no longer any reason to suppose that either of us had anything to do with it,' said Antony, deliberately misunderstanding.

'That's not what I meant, and I think you know it. It's bound to come out now that Veronica was guilty, and you say

187

you didn't want him to know.'

'No, and when I tell him what happened, which I don't propose to do until tomorrow morning, I shan't stress that fact. What I will do is to suggest that he should go and see Fran and tell her that though it may take a little time there's nothing more for her to worry about.'

'And if you'll tell me what time you're going to call him, I'll time myself to arrive at his office about ten minutes later,' said Meg. 'Unless you'd rather go, Jenny, the only thing is I think it should be just one of us.'

'I'd much rather you went,' said Jenny with feeling.

'All right. I shall try to talk some sense into him, and if I can manage it he'll propose to her before either of them know what really happened.'

Sir Nicholas sat up suddenly very straight in his chair. 'Match-making again?' he said, his eyes going from Meg to Jenny and then back to Meg again.

'It's in a good cause, Uncle Nick. You see if she accepts him before she knows Veronica's guilty it'll go some way to taking away the bad taste that Lynn left when he told her about his father.'

'Why not go about it in a straightforward manner?'

Jenny and Meg were still explaining that to him in chorus ten minutes later when Vera, seeing her husband's unprecedented look of confusion, interrupted them saying, 'I think it would be better if you left it to me to explain the matter when we're alone. After all, I think Antony's had enough of the subject for one evening, don't you?'

Epilogue

Maitland got home a little late the next evening. 'I had a call from Chief Inspector Sykes,' he told Jenny as he went into the living-room, but Jenny was not to be put off so easily from imparting her own news.

'Johnny's been here!' she said. 'In fact he only left a few minutes ago. He wanted to tell me that Meg had done the trick . . . of course that isn't how he put it. He probably never realised she'd been manoeuvring him. But he did propose to Fran, and he was accepted.'

'Did he tell her everything?'

'Yes, of course, he did. I don't know quite how Meg managed to persuade him that it wouldn't make any difference at all to someone who was really in love with him, but she seems to have done so. So I thought I'd better explain to him –'

'Yes, Jenny love?'

'Well, I do think this time I managed to be quite lucid. Anyway, he seemed to understand me. I thought he might take the detail of our little plot better from me.'

'I daresay you're quite right about that. What did he say?'

Jenny looked at him for a long moment. 'He laughed,' she said. 'He said he'd known all along what Veronica had done, and it had amused him to see you pussy-footing around the subject. And he'd been just as deceitful as we were really because he never told Fran what he thought about that, not until after she'd said she'd marry him.'

'I wonder if Uncle Nick understands it all yet,' said Antony.

He put his left arm around her shoulders and urged her towards the fireplace. When she moved away from him to take her usual place on the sofa he looked down at her and saw that her serene look, which had been missing for a day or two, was back in place. 'Your happy ending, love?' he said lightly.

She returned his gaze seriously. 'But not altogether for you, Antony,' she said, with an inquiring note in her voice.

'Oh yes, I suppose so.' But a moment later he was contradicting himself. 'You never met them, but I keep thinking of Maurice and Isabel Keats and how they're feeling tonight. And I also keep thinking how I tricked them, but even if I'd known where my questions were leading I don't see what else I could have done. Fran has her point of view, after all.'

'You said Inspector Sykes phoned you?'

'Yes. it was to say that Stephen Keats had been interviewed and had made a full confession. He lost his nerve when he discovered that the means of his grandfather's death were known, and he lost his nerve again today. He's under arrest and Fran will be released after a brief hearing in the morning.'

'Have you told Uncle Nick and Vera?'

'Yes, I stopped in the study on my way in. He gave me the usual lecture about not getting mixed up with the police, which I think he's been holding in reserve for days. But I think he was glad really.'

'Of course he was, and so was Vera.' Jenny broke off and stared at him for a moment. 'Antony, I've just had a dreadful thought,' she announced.

'My dearest love, it's over. You needn't have any more dreadful thoughts,' he told her.

'Perhaps, but that's not what this is,' said Jenny, not very coherently. 'Bernard Stanley is the Keats' family solicitor.'

'What of it?'

'If they take the case to him he'll hand it over to Geoffrey because he's the one who does all the criminal matters and has more experience,' said Jenny. 'And Geoffrey . . . you know he always wants you if it's a difficult case.'

190

'Well, this time he won't get me,' said Maitland very definitely. 'The whole thing was much too cold-blooded, probably plotted over a couple of years. I can't see that there's a single thing to be said in Stephen Keats's favour.'

But it was Meg who had the last word when she and Roger came to tea on Sunday. 'I'm thinking of giving up acting,' she said, 'and setting up a matrimonial agency instead. I'm sure I'd be a great success.'

If anything was needed to reconcile her husband to the continuation of her theatrical career, that was it. 'Not if I know it,' he said firmly. 'I'm glad Johnny and his Fran are happy, but that sort of interference can be carried too far.'